The Last Survivors

Book 1 of The Last Survivors Series
a collaboration by
Bobby Adair & T.W. Piperbrook

T.W. Piperbrook

Website: www.twpiperbrook.com
Facebook: www.facebook.com/twpiperbrook

Bobby Adair

Website: www.bobbyadair.com
Facebook: www.facebook.com/BobbyAdairAuthor

©2014 Beezle Publishing

Cover Design and Layout
Alex Saskalidis, a.k.a. 187designz

Editing & Proofreading
Cathy Moeschet

eBook and Print Formatting
Kat Kramer

Technical Consultant
John Cummings

Preface

Things would have been a lot simpler if I hadn't listened to Bobby Adair.

When I first approached him mid-Summer 2014, I told him I had an idea: we'd get together a few authors, and each of us would contribute a short story. When we were finished, we'd compile them in a small anthology and publish it around September or October, in between working on our other projects.

Before I knew it, Bobby had signed the two of us up for a full-scale novel. Which grew to a series. Which ended up being published sooner than either of us planned.

But hey, that's the fun of this whole writing thing, right?

Going into a collaboration is a scary endeavor. Unlike writing solo, where you have yourself to rely on (and blame), you're suddenly faced with the writing habits, imagination, and whims of your co-conspirator. For some, this might be a difficult task; for others, it might not work at all.

That wasn't the case at all with THE LAST SURVIVORS. From beginning to end, the ideas flowed, and they never stopped. And that is the reason you're holding this book several months earlier than we'd expected.

THE LAST SURVIVORS is different than anything I (or we) have ever written. It takes place in a post-apocalyptic setting where almost all of the technology of the modern world has been lost. The three townships, or last fragments of society, are plagued not only by internal dissent but also by monsters that roam the ruins and the forest. The science of the monsters is loosely based on the Cordyceps fungus, which exists today in tropical environments, primarily affecting insects such as ants. For those unfamiliar with the fungus, it simultaneously takes over and deforms the bodies of its hosts, taking control of their minds and afflicting them until death.

Because of the threat of wind-borne fungal spores and the loss of technology, the survivors in our story have devolved to a medieval, agrarian, almost-Puritanical culture. While they live in the ruins of modern cities, much of the past has been reduced to legend, and you are more likely to encounter a horse or a sword than any piece of modern "Tech Magic".

As you can tell, we took lots of liberties in our story. The world of THE LAST SURVIVORS is as much full of Fantasy as it is of science. We hope you have as much fun reading the book as we did writing it. Enjoy!

– Tyler Piperbrook

September 2014

Prologue

They were ugly.

They stank.

The disorganized horde of them was almost a mile down the slope, reeking a putrescence the boy could smell despite the direction of the breeze. Rot got into the misshapen, boney masses on their skulls and spines, making the creatures smell like decaying animals. They weren't dead, though. They were more than alive enough to chase a man down, eviscerate him, and feast on his entrails.

From atop his horse, the boy looked at the cloudless blue sky, then down the slope, and across the grassy, rolling hills, beautiful except for the thousands of dirty bare feet stomping them to dirt. "I'm frightened," he said.

General Blackthorn looked at his son and frowned. "Any boy of your age—most men in fact—would fear the sight of so many monsters afoot. But to admit that fear is a shameful thing." Blackthorn looked around, scanning the horizon. "Hearts harden under the hammer of fear, and yours will be no exception."

The boy scooted around in his saddle and looked behind the hilltop, where a dark forest brooded in shadows. "Are there more beasts hiding in the trees?"

Blackthorn pointed out across the thousands of running men, twisted by spore into rabid things, demonic things, hungry for the flesh of clean men. "No man has seen this many swarm out of the ancient city since the days when my grandfather was a boy. Do you truly imagine there could be more?"

The boy shook his head. It was a hope as much as a response.

Tales recounted by his father's soldiers around the hearths at night, stories he thought had been exaggerated to frighten a small boy, had proven true. Men were no longer men, but beasts. Beasts whose shoulders, spines and elbows grew bony, fungal warts, and whose skulls grew disfigured crests. Twice a year the crests plumed red, shedding spores into the wind, infecting humans, worming their way into the bones, sinking fungal roots and slowly deforming anyone unfortunate enough to be tainted.

Even a single wind-borne speck could fall on a tongue and mutate a person into a hideous monster. But the worst was that the spore twisted men's minds, transforming them into creatures who wallowed in their own feces, ate the flesh of other men, and stole away women to who knew what end.

Before the boy had seen the monsters, it'd been easy for him to show a brave face and beg his father to allow him to ride out with the cavalry. The boy was only fourteen, a year into his training. Normally riding in the cavalry was a privilege reserved for those of sixteen years of age at least.

But the boy was the son of General Blackthorn.

Now he'd give anything to be back behind the false safety of Brighton's walls.

Demon stench—a scent the boy had learned these past few days to fear—was growing around them, putrefying the wind, dripping over the scent of the wild summer flowers. Down the long grassy slope in front of the remains of the cavalry, the mass of the demon horde moved like some giant gelatinous slug, devouring the earth, fetid, with bulbous skulls and ten thousand hungry maws. Rotted teeth snapped on their wails while hands grasped air, reaching for the riders.

Blood was their lust.

General Blackthorn sat tall in his saddle, sneering as he looked down at the oncoming swarm, making the boy wonder if his father might have in him the strength to kill every last one of the monsters himself. The other riders waited stolidly for orders, men whose hard faces showed no fear. The boy ached to be as brave as his father—to be as brave as any of the cavalrymen—but it took all of his strength to hold himself steady on his horse. It took all of his courage to keep from wetting his pants.

He waited, anticipating what was to come. But that was no mental feat. The cavalry did only one thing—it charged as though the men knew no fear, as though their comrades hadn't been mauled and killed by the dozen, by the tens of dozens. Of the six hundred cavalrymen that rode out of Brighton three days prior and had valiantly fought mobs and bands of spore-infected men across the countryside, only seventy-five were left.

The boy knew, just as the surviving men knew, that they wouldn't live to see their homes again. It was a realization that had come to each of them as each bloody day passed. But not one of the soldiers had complained, nor had they admitted their fear.

As the boy looked back and forth across the cavalry aligned beside him, he saw their hard hands gripping their reins and hefting their swords. Individually and together, they projected indomitable strength.

And through his growing panic, the boy understood something new that he'd been clueless about through all the previous days' slaughter. Fear itself was not a shameful thing. Admitting one's fear for the ears of other men dampened their courage. That was the shame. Understanding that, the boy gritted his teeth, sat up straight in his saddle and looked down at the stinking swarm. In his strongest voice, he said, "Father, I'm ready to fight."

Blackthorn looked at the boy, and for the first time since they'd ridden out of Brighton, his face softened. "I'm proud of you, my son."

"I'm proud of you, too, father." The boy's voice cracked, and he dared say no more.

Blackthorn waved his arm and gave the order. The horsemen formed up in a chevron of fifty riders with Blackthorn at the point. The other twenty-five riders fell in behind.

The cavalry charged.

Every bulbous-headed monster in the swarm screamed defiance at the horses thundering down on them.

Bone broke under hoof.

Blood gushed under blade.

Demons shrieked, and men fell.

The horses lost momentum, stuck in the solid mob of beasts. Without the charging mass of twelve hundred-pound horses trampling twisted men, the cavalrymen were left with only the strength of their swords. The attack fell apart.

Men and horses succumbed to clawing hands and jagged teeth. General Blackthorn tried in vain to rally the soldiers, but fear had a grip on too many hearts. Amidst the reeking bodies, desperation came easily.

The boy swung at a nearby monster, catching it across the neck. Blood gushed. The beast fell. Off to his left, the General was swinging his sword. Demons were yanking at his tunic, tugging on his arms, grasping at his horse's bridle.

Then something occurred that the boy had never thought possible. General Blackthorn fell. He was instantly buried in a scrum of a dozen beasts.

The brave, iron hearts of the cavalrymen crumbled.

The boy's own fear won out, and he kicked his horse in the haunches, spurring it into a panicked gallop back toward the hill. Monsters fell to the side as the horse picked up speed through the melee. The boy swung his sword—not to kill, but simply to fend off the monsters and escape.

While the boy was still swinging wildly, the horse broke out of the horde, and flew through the knee-high grass toward the hill they'd charged down earlier. He wiped at his tear-streaked face, feeling shame for leaving his comrades behind. When he looked back though, he saw several dozen bloodied horsemen racing after him. And his father's great black horse among them, riderless.

At the top of the hill the boy slowed, stopped, and turned his horse around to look back on some wispy false hope that he might see his father on his feet, slaying the beasts. Of course he wasn't. General Blackthorn was dead.

The other fleeing horsemen came to a stop and wheeled their horses up alongside the boy. With his cheeks still wet with blood and tears he looked over the men. His father's second in command was gone. No officer was among them. Even the sergeants had all fallen. The horsemen were leaderless and they were all staring at him. The boy had seen those looks before, while he'd been mounted at his father's side. Now the cavalrymen were looking for his direction, for his leadership. The mantle of the general had passed a weight onto his shoulders that threatened to splinter his fearful bones.

The man on the horse next to the boy stood up in his saddle and looked back and forth across the thin, ragged formation. "The men are prepared to charge, sir."

They were ready to fight, ready to resume a battle they'd already lost, ready to die.

But the cavalrymen couldn't fail. If they did, there'd be no one to stop the horde from reaching Brighton, no one to stop the beasts from pouring over the walls and slaughtering everyone the boy ever knew.

Rather than despair, though that choice begged him to spur his horse into a gallop far away from here, the boy asked himself what his father would do? Form a chevron and bravely charge into the teeth of the deformed brutes.

The words ran through the boy's head as if they were his own. General Blackthorn had always sworn by one tactic, and according to General Blackthorn, that tactic was all they needed. A wall of charging horses invariably put fear in the hearts of demons, and fear made the beasts turn and run. That made them easy to slay.

But the horde down in the prairie was large enough to absorb any quantity of fear the boy's few charging horses could engender.

"Sir?" the man next to the boy asked, waiting for an answer.

The boy's mind raced. He formed an idea. He stood in his saddle and trotted a few steps ahead of the cavalry lined along the crest. Swallowing his fear, he looked at the men. "The chevron will be useless with so few riders against so many monsters."

The man who'd been next to him was unable to hide his unease. "But we know only one way to fight the beasts."

"Quiet. Hear what he has to say," said another man.

"I have an idea. But you'll need to follow me with faith and courage." The men quietly listened. "My father is dead. Our brothers are dead. We are exhausted, and our horses are tired. But if we give up now, all of your wives and children will die. Is that what we want?"

The men stared at him in silence.

The boy yelled, "Is that what we want?"

In unison, the men cried, "No!"

The boy continued, his confidence rising. "We will not win this battle. We all know that. But we will fight until the last of us falls. And in dying, we will kill so many demons that by the time they reach the walls of Brighton, there will be so few that the women and children will finish them with their kitchen tools. Will you follow me? Will you ride behind me?"

The men cheered.

"Form a single line! Do as I do!"

The boy wheeled his horse around. He looked down the hill at an advancing mass of grunting beasts. His heart thudded in his chest, but he fought to harden it, doing as his father would've done. He gritted his teeth, he held up his sword. Then he gave the command. His horse whinnied as he raced down the slope. The wind caressed his face, drying the blood that stained his cheeks. He kept his stare straight ahead. He didn't look to see if the men had followed. They were good cavalrymen, his father's men.

The horde drew closer.

When the boy reached the bottom of the hill, he didn't charge the center like his father would have. Instead, he led the line of horsemen along the flank, slicing his sword at every outstretched monster hand, every shoulder, every neck. When the monsters moved into his path, he skirted around them. He didn't engage them in combat. He didn't even slow his horse. The horsemen followed his lead, slashing at demon limbs as they rode.

When he'd ridden well past the swarm, the boy brought his horse to a stop. He looked left and right, assessing the scene. He asked the man next to him, "How many did we lose?"

"Not a one, sir."

He felt a surge of hope. The horde was shrieking and changing direction to give chase.

"Which way to Brighton?" the boy asked.

The soldier pointed to the left, back in the direction of the hillock.

The boy stood in his saddle, addressing his troops. "We'll attack them on the opposite flank and draw them away from our homes. These stinking things are slower than our horses and dumber than our pigs. We don't need to battle them for our honor. We need to slaughter them like hogs."

The men hollered, and without hesitation, the boy led another harassing charge.

The men whooped into the air, battling behind him until their swords were stained and their muscles weak. For two days, they fought, repeating the maneuver until the horde had thinned.

At the end of the second day, half the demons in the great horde were dead on the prairie.

By that time, the remaining men in the boy's command were weary and out of strength. Their heads hung; their swords were heavy in their hands. But something was approaching on the horizon. A troop of a hundred farmers had arrived on horseback, offering reinforcement. Without question, the men fell in line with the soldiers, rallying behind the boy.

Rallying behind the new leader. The new General Blackthorn.

Chapter 1: Ella

"William, where are you?"

Ella scanned the trees in a panic. A few minutes earlier, she'd been talking with her eleven-year-old son about the town gathering, discussing the things they'd do after The Cleansing. William had been watching her, wide-eyed and intent, barely interested in the mint leaves and roots they'd been collecting.

And now he was gone.

She'd preached the necessity of staying close, had warned him of the dangers. The forest wasn't safe. How many times could she have said it?

You'd think he would've learned, after what happened to his father...

But there was no time to think about that now. She dropped her bag, grabbed the folds of her skirt, and lifted them so she could run. Then she drew her knife.

As she ran, her boots grappled with rocks and fallen branches, the trees seemed to surround her. A few moments ago, the forest had seemed tranquil and inviting, but not anymore.

The panic was taking over.

"William!" she shouted again, louder this time.

They'd been out since early in the morning and already the sun was spreading its heat through the foliage, the light dappling with shadows.

Was William hiding, playing one of his silly games?

If so, he'd be in deep trouble. He knew better. She'd taught him better.

She flew past several mulberry trees, her breath coming in short bursts. Tree limbs scratched painfully at her arms. Brambles tore at her skirt. Where was William?

It was her fault. They shouldn't have gone so far into the forest. Even though they were inside the circle wall, that didn't mean they were safe. The wall, ancient and long, was crumbling in places and was only guarded at the gates.

A shape appeared in the distance. Even through the glare and shadow, she recognized her son's form. His long arms whisked back and forth; his pants billowed behind him.

"William! Stop!"

She ran faster, pushing her legs to the point of cramping. Her heart pounded. Her stomach turned end over end.

Why was William running? Why wouldn't he stop? She scanned the forest—left, right, and behind—but saw nothing. What had spooked him?

Had he seen something she hadn't?

Whatever it was, she'd protect him from it. She'd do whatever it took to keep him safe. William was all she had left.

She kept on, ignoring the stitches in her side. Her lungs heaved for air. Her legs begged for respite. Run. Faster.

A sound rose from the forest.

A child's voice.

It was William, and he was calling out to someone. Who was he talking to?

She looked around as she ran, trying to keep pace with William's wild strides. He darted between trees, leaping over brush. She shouted again, with as much volume as she could muster.

William ground to a halt, as if her voice had snapped him from some animal trance. His shoulders rose and fell as he turned and faced her.

"Where do you think you're going?"

William stared at her, but didn't answer. She continued toward him. With each footstep, her anxiety faded. In its place grew a swell of anger.

"Don't ever do that to me again! You hear me?"

She opened her mouth to scold him further, but stopped when she saw the guilty look on his face. His curly brown hair clung to his forehead; his eyes roamed the forest floor. She took him by the shoulders, softening her tone.

"Why'd you take off like that, William? Are you trying to get yourself killed?"

William didn't answer. He kept his eyes on the ground.

"Look at me when I speak to you!" Ella demanded.

The boy refused, and she felt her anger return. Her son had disobeyed her. On top of that, he wouldn't even dignify his behavior with an explanation. If he didn't answer her soon, she'd—

"I saw Dad."

Ella's face went slack. In the second between question and response, the boy met her eyes. She stared at her son's face, hoping to rekindle her anger, but all she felt was sorrow. Ethan—the boy's father—had died almost a year ago.

Her eyes welled up as she studied William.

Her husband was gone, but reminders of him were alive in her son—his nose, his mouth, his jaw line.

"Daddy's gone, honey." She tried to control the waver in her voice. "You know that. We both know that."

"But I saw him. He was waving at me through the trees."

Ella stared past him. The forest was quiet and still.

Of course Ethan wasn't out there. She'd watched him burn.

"It wasn't him, William."

"But I—"

"Remember what Daddy said? Remember how he told us to be strong, like the others?"

William nodded. She could see the memory pass through his face. It was the same memory she'd clung to since Ethan had died—the one that had helped her through many sleepless nights. The one that had helped assuage her guilt, pulling her out of the dark depression that had threatened to consume her.

It was better to remember Ethan's final words than to think of his last moments: the torches, the fire, the crackle of his burnt skin. The chanting of the townsfolk as they drowned out his screams, sending him off to whatever god they believed in.

She'd stopped believing in anything that day.

Sure, she still said the words when everyone else said the words. She listened to Father Winthrop. She nodded. She knelt. She mimicked the motions of hands. But she'd disconnected the meanings from the sounds, the faith from reality, and she'd given up on her old beliefs.

The only thing keeping her alive now was William.

She looked back at her son. His eyes drifted across the landscape, as if hoping the forest would reveal his father. His face was stained with tears, and she realized her face was wet, too. "I'm sorry, sweetie," she said.

He opened his mouth to speak, but his lips quivered and closed. She pulled him against her, letting him bury his head in her shoulder, trying to fill the gap his father had left behind. If only Ethan had been more careful.

If only he hadn't been infected...

She brushed her hands through her son's hair, doing her best to console him. His muffled sobs drifted between the trees, and his thin gasps stabbed at her heart. She rubbed his back.

Then she felt it.

Ella's hands stopped moving, and her breath lodged in her throat. Was she imagining things now? She moved her eyes from his back to the forest, as if it would reveal some clue, some proof that she was in a new nightmare.

But she wasn't. At least, she didn't think she was. She could feel her son breathing in her embrace, and she could feel the thud of two heartbeats between them.

She moved her fingers again on his back, slowly this time, hoping she'd been mistaken. But the lump was still there, at the base of his neck. Calcified, knotted, and ugly. Just like Ethan's had been.

Her heart seized in her chest.

The boy hadn't been imagining things, after all.

He'd been delusional, but for a reason.

"No," she whispered, closing her eyes. "Not my son."

Chapter 2: Father Winthrop

"Why do we Cleanse only the women and children?"

Father Winthrop looked at the boy, reconsidering his decision not to beat him. He turned to his elder novice. "Franklin, the boy is tiring me. Tell him the words."

"Yes, Father."

"You and the boy dress yourselves," said Father Winthrop, "The Cleansing awaits."

Franklin bent down, picking up Oliver's pants and pressing them into the boy's hands. "Put them on."

Oliver looked down at his naked body, turned his elbow up for a better view, and rotated his wrists slowly in front of his face. "I'm clean, right?"

"Yes," Franklin answered.

That was one of the things that continually impressed Father Winthrop about Franklin. He was always patient with the boy. Indeed, he was patient with all of the ignorant townsfolk. That patience extended into a talent for planting knowledge and cultivating thought in the barren soil of their minds. He'd even shown a special aptitude for turning their pointless questions back on them in an effort to make them understand how all things good stemmed from the virtues of The Word.

On the other hand, Oliver, as dim-witted as he was, was only half as ignorant as the dirt scratchers and pig chasers who put their butts on the benches morning after morning, moon after moon. There was still hope he could be trained.

After finishing with his clothes, Franklin began his recital of the words Father Winthrop had taught him. "The hearts of men are hard as stone. The man has no need of the tear. The man has no need of the lie. The man has no weakness. The man kills. The man dies. That is the boon and the burden of the man."

Leaving the two at the top undone, Oliver fastened the remaining buttons on his shirt. He swung his hands down to his sides.

"Come here, Oliver." Franklin smiled and reached over to button the last two.

Oliver looked up at him. "But I like them unbuttoned."

Franklin shook his head.

Ignoring the issue of Oliver's buttons, Father Winthrop put the boys back on track. "Where were we, Franklin? The subject of women next, I believe."

"Women are weak," Franklin droned. "Women must be weak to love a baby enough to hold it to their breast. Women's hearts must be weak to sacrifice for their children. Women must be weak to take the seed of the man. Because women are weak, a woman cannot keep the truth. Love triumphs over truth. So a woman's words are lies."

"Wait a minute," Oliver interrupted again. "Women lie and men do not?"

"Yes," Franklin replied.

Already distracted from what they'd been talking about, Oliver turned to look through the window at the nervous crowd outside.

"Listen, Oliver," Franklin said. "You need to know this. Okay?"

Oliver refocused and smiled.

Maybe Oliver really IS simple, Father Winthrop thought, reconsidering his earlier position. If I hadn't promised the boy's father just before the man died, I'd probably turn him out to the field.

With the boys finished dressing, Father Winthrop walked to the door and the boys followed.

"I don't understand," Oliver said to Franklin, as they approached the door. "We're men. Why do we have to be Cleansed?"

"When boys age seventeen years, their hearts become hard like stone. Until then, boys are not men. They are not women either. But they cannot be trusted. They must be Cleansed. Father Winthrop Cleanses us. The only people excused from the ceremony are men who are of age and too busy with their work. You know this, Oliver."

Oliver stopped and put his hands on his hips. "But that's what I don't understand."

Father Winthrop swung the heavy wooden door open. His patience was at an end. In a voice harsher than usual, he asked, "What is it, Oliver? What don't you understand?"

"Why can't a husband Cleanse his wife and children the way you have Cleansed us?"

Father Winthrop looked at Franklin, redirecting the question.

"Um—"

Father Winthrop shook his head. "You should know this, Franklin."

"I don't remember the words."

"As long as you know the meaning, the exact phrasing isn't necessary. Not yet."

Father Winthrop looked at Oliver. "The weakness of a woman can soften the stone of a man's heart. In soft stone, lies can live."

"You mean men can lie?" Oliver asked.

Father Winthrop shook his head. "Outside with you."

The boys proceeded through the door.

Walking on, Father Winthrop added, "Best not to let the temptations of a woman soften the stone of a man's heart. Not all men can resist a woman who urges him to lie."

"Why?" Oliver asked again.

"You'll see when you get older," Franklin told him, as though it were a secret.

The pair ascended the stairs on their elder's heels. Once on the dais, Father Winthrop crossed a dozen steps and greeted the two men already seated there. "General Blackthorn. Minister Beck."

"Good of you to finally arrive, Father." Minister Beck smirked when he said it.

Ignoring the jab, Father Winthrop ensconced himself in his chair to the left of General Blackthorn. He looked out over the thousands of women. Some had children's hands clutching at their skirts; a few were too old to have children young enough for Cleansing. The men of the township were not in the crowd around the Cleansing stone that stood at the center of the square. A few lingered along the edges, standing near their wives. Most were perched on rooftops or hung out of windows, silently watching, judging. But, Father Winthrop suspected, mostly lusting.

Murmurs ran through the crowd. They shuffled more than usual. They were nervous.

Along with Minister Beck and General Blackthorn, Father Winthrop had presided over the ritual twice annually for thirteen years. In that time, he'd learned to read the mood. Either they could sense the unclean or smudged among them, or they'd seen for themselves when a shameless one of them had exposed her soiled skin. When that happened, the chasers and scratchers never came forward. But the rumors would spread. They'd hide in the crowd, hoping to mask their secret in their numbers.

They didn't know their nervousness told their secret to anyone who was paying attention.

Didn't they know they were endangering everyone in the township? Maybe the selfish dullards didn't care.

Franklin took up his position behind Father Winthrop. Oliver stood next to him.

An armed man walked across the platform and stopped in front of General Blackthorn. "Shall we begin, General?"

"Yes. Please," answered Blackthorn.

The armed man turned to face the thousands in the square. "Begin The Cleansing."

The women and children fell silent.

A white stone platform stood just a few dozen feet in front of the dais—ten feet long, with stone steps leading up on one side and down on the other. At the foot of the stairs three tables had been erected. Behind those were the takers of the Cleansing census, whose job it was to ensure all the women and children in the township came forward and were counted.

A woman approached the bottom of the stairs. She'd already disrobed, and she handed her clothes to a young girl next to her. One of the census takers scribbled something in a book.

The woman stared straight ahead, her eyes wide and vacant. She climbed the steps to the top of the platform. She crossed to the center and raised her arms, then spun slowly, no expression on her face.

The crowd looked on in silence. Each knew their turn was coming.

After a full rotation, the woman proceeded toward the stairs at the other side of the platform, where several men in white waited to inspect her more closely. They went to work with practiced hands, examining her body not just for color, not just for warts that protruded, but also for the unnatural hardness of the unclean bumps before they made themselves visible.

Another naked woman—a young, shapely girl of no more than sixteen—walked up the steps on the other side of the platform and the process proceeded.

Father Winthrop heard Franklin's breath quicken behind him. He turned and whispered over his shoulder. "Don't let your lust blind you to the gravity of our duty here, my son. For the preservation of all, we must ensure that these weak women are clean."

Chapter 3: Ella

"Where are we going, Mom?" William asked, his eyes wide.

Ella didn't answer. She continued stuffing the belongings from their house into two bags, her mind spitting thoughts faster than she could process them.

"William, get me the water flasks from the storeroom."

"Why?"

"Do it now, William."

"But—"

"I mean it. No more questions."

William opened his mouth to protest, but snapped it shut when he saw the look on her face. She watched him dart across the room and to a smaller room on the other side. Ella returned to the bag. She tried to envision what was going on at the town center, but the image only frightened her further.

Relax. They're probably just starting the line. You have plenty of time to pack, plenty of time to leave. No one will notice until you're gone—

"Mom? I can't find the flasks."

"They're over by the drying board."

The line will take most of the afternoon. The women will climb the steps when the sun hits its apex—

"I don't see them."

"They're there, William!"

—and then they'll spin in a circle and move to the inspectors. And then—

"I still can't find them."

"William! Dammit!"

Ella stood up and flung the bag against one of the stone walls. The contents spilled to the floor, blankets falling into heaps and herbs into misshapen piles. She buried her head in her hands and started to sob.

William fled the storeroom and knelt by her side, his hands tight on her arm. "What's wrong, Mom?"

"I'm sorry, honey. It's not your fault," she managed, between the tears. She lifted her head and blotted her face with the sleeves of her dress. "We just need to hurry."

"Why? Where are we going?"

"I told you. We're taking a trip."

"Won't they miss us at The Cleansing?"

She looked into his face, wishing she could will away the years of ritual and lies that had been implanted in his brain. But they were already ingrained in him, hidden behind innocent eyes, adhered to his memory. The Cleansing was as much a part of him as it was of her.

I don't care what they think! I don't care what they do! Ella wanted to scream.

Instead, she replied calmly. "I've cleared it with Father Winthrop. We'll be fine."

If they were caught, she'd take the blame. She'd even jump into the fire first, if she needed to. Anything to protect her son.

She collected both her belongings and her thoughts, tucking them away for later. Then she walked William over to the storeroom, locating the flasks. They were right where she'd put them, placed between the drying board and a sack of grain.

She tucked the flasks and some food into the two bags, tested the weights of each, and handed him the lighter one.

"Here you go, William."

He slipped the bag over his shoulder. It hung from his back like a second body, and she found herself thinking how small he was for his age. Eleven years old and barely as tall as his peers, too skinny for chickenball and too short for the gridiron.

And now he'll never live to play those games.

STOP IT, ELLA.

She stared at the boy, envisioning the lumps underneath his clothes. How many were there? She still hadn't had time to do a full inspection.

Even one lump was enough to convict him.

She'd been tight-lipped since she'd discovered it. There was no need to alarm him. She wasn't even sure if the boy knew what was happening.

"Come on, sweetie," she said, tugging his hand.

When they reached the door, she took a last look behind her. The room was virtually empty. Two bedrolls sat on the floor, stripped of their sheets. The storeroom door hung open in the corner.

The place looked vacant already. They hadn't had much to begin with.

She wondered how long it would take for her house to be auctioned. When the officials discovered her gone, they'd seize the rest of her belongings and sell them to the highest-bidding merchant. Perhaps some street dweller would scrape up enough silver to purchase her small home. Her eyes welled up at the prospect of losing it. She'd built it with Ethan.

In just a year, she'd lost everything—her husband, her home, and her faith.

They won't get my son.

William squeezed her hand, as if sensing the urgency of their mission, and she turned to face the door. Before opening it, she glanced at the four-foot tapestry on the wall. A gift from Ethan. A wedding present. She wanted to take it, but it was too large to carry. They'd need to travel light, if they were to have any chance at reaching Davenport.

She glanced at it one last time, remembering the last words Ethan had spoken to her after he'd instructed them to be strong.

"Whatever you do, Ella, protect our son."

That was before they'd lit the torch, before they'd set his body afire. She swallowed another round of tears and reached for the door handle.

I'll protect him, Ethan. I swear.

***

The dirt-covered streets—normally filled with men's pushcarts—were now empty. The vegetable and merchant stands had been packed up and secured, the doors to the buildings had been locked, the children collected. She pulled William along, casting nervous glances at back alleys and doorways, as if the townsfolk had already deciphered their plan and were ready to ambush them.

She knew how vicious people could be, especially around the time of The Cleansing.

Over the years, she'd seen brothers turn against sisters, men turn against wives, and mothers turn against sons. That was the code, and that was what was expected of them.

Loyalty was cast aside for the greater good.

At least, that's what the townsfolk always said, after the fires had died down and the scent of burnt flesh had dissipated.

"There was nothing we could've done. We did what we had to do," they always reasoned.

Bullshit, Ella thought.

If she could rewind time back to Ethan's death, she'd have done it all differently. She'd have forced her husband to flee. She'd have started over. The infection wouldn't have turned him right away — in fact, if the whispers of the old women were to be believed, it might never have turned him at all. Surely they could've had more time together.

In some ways, she would've preferred that Ethan had become one of the demons than be burned on the pyre. As bloodthirsty as the beasts were, at least they weren't hypocrites. They didn't preach one thing and do another. They didn't force people to betray their spouses, or force mothers to Cleanse in front of their sons.

Even if she were caught, at least Ella would be spared the humiliation of standing on the dais one last time, spinning and turning, wishing she could disappear, while William watched.

She'd rather be condemned than do it again.

Beside her, William faltered, and she caught his arm in time to prevent a fall. In her haste, she'd been pulling him faster than his legs could run. She slowed.

"Sorry, honey," she whispered. "But you have to keep up with Mommy."

They dashed through the empty streets, their footsteps reverberating off of buildings and doorways. Normally, the townsfolk would fill them up, laughing, drinking, fighting and cajoling. But not today.

Ella took a circuitous route to the town's edge, hoping to stay as far away from the town center as possible.

The guards would be watching. Especially today.

It would make sense that the infected would flee beforehand, but that wasn't always the case. Many of the unclean stayed until the last minute, unable to pry themselves from relatives and friends. It was a mistake that always cost them their lives.

If only Ella had discovered William's lump sooner.

Keep moving.

There was no way to change the past. There was only time to react to it. She pulled William along, her feet already sore. She'd been meaning to procure new boots from the cobbler, but she hadn't gotten the chance.

Now she'd be forced to deal with the pain.

As they ran, the gleam of washed stone gave way to the growth of untended weeds. The sight gave her a tinge of relief. The overgrowth meant she was leaving the town center. She'd need to keep an eye out for the guards.

She cut across several alleyways, leaving behind the northern section and entering the town's outer limits. She glanced at the buildings as she ran by them, soaking them in for the last time, absorbing the memories of years gone by.

A shout shook her back to the present. William's hand had tightened in hers, and she pulled him into a nearby alley for cover. She flattened her back against the building, beckoning him to do the same.

She maintained the position for several seconds, her chest heaving. Tall weeds poked through the cracks in the masonry and tickled her neck. Beside her, she could hear the thin rasps of her son, and when she looked at him, she saw his eyes darting left and right down the narrow alley.

How long did he have? Would it be days? Months? Weeks?

When would the hallucinations take over?

Stop it.

She swallowed and focused on the footsteps, trying to pinpoint their location. Shouts rang out again. This time they were closer, and she fought the urge to peek around the corner.

She held fast to her hiding place, praying they hadn't been seen. The guards were fast and well trained—once they were spotted, there'd be no outrunning them. They'd be dragged to the town center and thrown to the head of the line.

There was a special place for people who betrayed The Word.

She glanced down the alley. The wall stretched fifty more feet. No doors or windows in sight.

The voices were almost upon them…

Please don't let this be the end…

"Marigold!" someone shouted. "Hurry!'

Ella glanced to the left in time to see a young boy and girl flying past them, heading in the direction of the town center. Their faces were red and winded; their feet pummeled the pavement.

"We're going to be late! I told you we didn't have time!"

"I'm sorry, David! It's my fault!"

The girl spoke in a nervous, high-pitched tone, as if she were on the verge of tears. Within seconds the pair was gone, and all at once, it was just Ella and William again, alone in their mission.

"Come on!" she urged William, without pausing to think.

They darted back to the main road, sticking close to doorways and alleys, avoiding the center of the thoroughfare. Before long, the buildings grew sparse, and she saw a line of trees in the distance nearly a mile across a wide field. Out there, she knew, was a part of the circle wall covered in overgrowth, a spot where they could get up it and over.

All the kids knew about it. Did the guards?

There was no time to speculate.

They dashed into the sunlight, feet plowing through knee-high grass, and fixed their eyes on the wall. The stones were mossed and worn, as if the wall had long ago ceased being a barrier and become a part of nature.

She fixed her eyes on a large oak. It'd been years since she'd been there, but the knots and gnarls had barely changed. There'd be an arrangement of loose stones in the side of the wall just beneath its branches, not enough to draw the naked eye, but enough to provide support for hands and feet.

She had no idea if the stones would hold. She'd never seen anyone climb them all the way up to the top.

She reached the wall and slid her hands over it, her fingernails catching on ratty weeds. Where was the first handhold? It used to be four feet from the ground.

Now it was gone.

This can't be.

Was she looking in the right place? Was it possible the stone had been removed? She hadn't been here in years. Anything could've happened in that time.

She continued groping the wall, moving left and right, glancing up at the oak every so often to keep her bearings. Nothing. No handholds. No footholds. No stone.

She looked at the top of the wall, which was about twenty-five feet high. She tried jumping and snagging hold of it, but slid uselessly back down. Even if she could find purchase and make it over, William would be stuck on this side.

The guards would find them soon.

Her whole plan had been useless. Insane.

Even if they tried to get back in time for the ceremony, there was no way they'd make it. Things were already underway, and a late entrance would draw even more suspicion. The townsfolk would find out William's secret—her secret—and then they'd both burn.

She choked back a sob and sank to her knees, the reality of the situation threatening to bowl her over. She'd done her best. She'd tried what she could.

I'm sorry, Ethan.

When the ceremony was over, they'd send search parties to look for her. There'd be no avoiding what was coming next. Ella cried softly into her hands, feeling defeated, guilty, and hopeless all at the same time. Through her tears, she heard the thin scrape of William's boots next to her, and she did her best to compose herself. He was probably scuffing the ground with his shoes, as he did when he got nervous. She needed to be a mother to him. No matter what came next, William was here now.

She opened her eyes and blotted her face, ready to provide comfort to the anxious boy. Only William wasn't anxious at all. The sound she'd heard wasn't the scratch of boots on turf, but the scrape of his body against the stone.

William was climbing the wall.

"Look, Mom!" he called. "I found a way up!"

She glanced up in shock, watching him place one unsteady foot above the other. The bag still hung from his shoulder.

"Be careful, honey!" she warned, her desperation turning to hope. "I'm coming up behind you!"

She adjusted her own bag and followed the path of his feet, locating the first handhold, then a place to wedge her boot. He'd found it! She tried to contain her excitement, focusing on pulling herself up the wall's slippery face.

Little by little, they gained distance from the ground, leaving the grass and the ruins behind. The next time they planted their feet, they'd be outside the town limits.

They'd be one step closer to escape, one step closer to a new life.

William was several feet ahead of her, approaching the top. She hissed at him to be careful. His bag swung back and forth on his shoulder, as if the contents themselves were aching for freedom.

She was so focused on the climb that she almost didn't hear the footsteps on the dirt below them. When she processed the sound, her blood froze. She looked up at William, but he kept climbing, oblivious to the disturbance.

A voice rang out.

"What do you think you're doing?"

"Get off of there, now!"

In mere moments, her hope had been destroyed.

The guards had found them.

Chapter 4: Minister Beck

Minister Beck watched a young blonde girl step up onto the Cleansing platform.

After seeing so many women that day, he thought he was past the initial physical stimulation of nudity. But her beauty sparkled beyond the usual standards by which such things were measured.

Crossing his legs to hide his embarrassment—after all, men were supposed to be above temptation—he admired the curve of her back and the way it widened so perfectly down to her buttocks. Her long corn silk hair hadn't even darkened in her private place. Beck smiled. Even in his thoughts, he was unwittingly bound by Father Winthrop's admonition against using the vulgar word to describe it. Realizing he was smiling, he faked a cough to cover that. A smile wasn't an appropriate facial expression while sitting in front of so many whose lives might be called to an end.

The utter perfection of the girl caused Beck to wonder if beauty weren't intangible, as many a song had insisted, but merely a natural proportion—a figure pleasing to the eye, like the petals of a flower. And of course, proportion itself was just a physical expression of mathematics. Beck wondered if he could task Scholar Evan, his mathematician, to initiate that study. He discarded that thought with a sigh. The Council of Elders would never approve. It never did.

Every suggestion Beck made for the sake of learning something new or rediscovering an ancient secret was derided. Practicality. That was the wish and the order of the Elders. A hotter fire to smelt old metals into their constituents. An arrow to fly more true. A means to seal the bucket on a water wheel to make it leak less. Those were things a simple mind could understand.

But exploring a way to save a crop from the grasshopper plague? That was simply against the will of God, according to Father Winthrop. Never to be explored.

Even worse was to suggest the possibility that The Cleansing could be avoided by protecting the townsfolk from the spore. The spore came twice a year. Everybody knew that. But covering one's face with a cloth for those days when the tiny red specks floated in the sunshine was never enough. People had tried that for centuries, only to see their hopes dashed. In the end, they accepted that it was the will of God, and did nothing except listen to Father Winthrop beg for mercies from above.

Beck watched the Cleansing Inspectors on the platform pet their hands across the blonde beauty's skin, conducting the final test for smudges and warts. He wondered what lusty fantasies engorged their thoughts when their fingers were on the naked skin of pretty young virgins. He envied them their task. Sure, they had hard hearts, but they had other parts as well.

Behind the young beauty, at the center of the platform, a wrinkled crone displayed rolls and dimples earned through years of gluttony. As she slowly spun for all to see, Beck's envy evaporated. He especially didn't envy the two children climbing the platform stairs, waiting their turn to be inspected.

"Beg your pardon, Ministers, General."

Beck startled and sat up in his chair.

A man, one of the rabbit hunters, came up onto the dais and approached the chairs where the three Elders sat, presiding. The rabbit hunter came to a stop and looked from the general to the ministers as though seeking some direction. Two armed guards, one on either side of the Elders, watched the rabbit hunter, but neither appeared to be concerned. The rabbit hunter's purpose was known to all. Men came to the dais on Cleansing day for only one reason. They had good hearts of stone. Or at least, that's what Winthrop would have them think.

Beck didn't believe any of Winthrop's mindless hokum. Superstitions were for peasants, not educated men. The rabbit hunter was on the dais because he didn't want the fire to lick his skin while he burned in the pyre. He didn't want his friends and children to think him a coward. He didn't want them to hear his screams. He wanted the easy way out.

General Blackthorn was always terse. "Speak."

"General—" The man's voice caught in his throat. He looked down at his feet and fidgeted with his belt buckle.

"My son." Father Winthrop leaned forward in his chair. "The fact that you are here proves your bravery. You need not be nervous."

The man's name was Muldoon. Beck recognized him, though grief seemed to have aged him by a decade in the past half year. His wife had been taken at the last Cleansing with a line of warts on her spine. The old men who sat in the square and played their board games said it was the fastest they'd seen the warts grow in years. Beck speculated that, in truth, she'd found a way to hide her uncleanliness from the town, from the inspectors, on previous days of Cleansing. But the warts had become too ugly and bulbous. They always did. Always. On the day of the last Cleansing, when she dropped her dress, the warts were clear, red, ugly, and hard on her back, some the size of a toddler's fist. Even an old woman with clouded eyes could see them.

And now, here was her widower husband, ready to pay the price for his collusion. Surely he had known about his wife's warts. But that only underscored the need for The Cleansing. People rarely came forth on their own to admit their disease. They needed to be compelled.

"I'm smudged," Muldoon said, without looking up.

"Where?" Father Winthrop asked.

The man pointed a thumb over his shoulder. "My back."

General Blackthorn leaned forward. "Smudged? How do you know that, if it's on your back? Did your son tell you?"

The man was stuck between words. He looked like he was hiding something.

"Out with it, man!" demanded General Blackthorn.

Muldoon looked left and right, then over his shoulder. "I was working."

In a softer tone, Father Winthrop said, "Go on."

"I had my shirt off. I was helping my cousin put hay in his barn. It was hot."

"And?"

"My cousin's neighbor, Earl Friend saw it."

"Earl Friend, the poultry man?"

"Yes."

Nodding knowingly, Father Winthrop said, "A man with a heart of stone. A good man to tell another such a sad thing. We're lucky to have such men."

Muldoon looked around again and checked over his shoulder.

"Is there more?" General Blackthorn asked, suspicion in his tone.

Muldoon nodded.

"Speak." Father Winthrop curled his fingers, trying to lure the words from the man's mouth.

"Earl Friend offered me comfort."

"How so?" Blackthorn asked.

Beck was getting curious. On a day of drudgery and tears, this minor mystery was a welcome distraction.

Muldoon looked at his feet when he spoke. He was ashamed. "He said he was smudged, too."

Blackthorn sat up straight, looking around, ready to put a spike in someone's head.

Had a snail been crawling on Father Winthrop's tongue his face could not have shown more disgust.

Beck asked, "And he was hiding it?"

Muldoon nodded.

"How long has he been hiding it?"

"Three Cleansings. Earl told me that if I said nothing, nothing would come of it. He said silence was a more powerful Cleanser than the pain of the pyre. He said a true man of The Word keeps his secret and disappears into the forest when the warts come. He said that's why so few men burn."

Beck shook his head. It was not going to go well for Earl Friend.

Father Winthrop turned to Blackthorn. "This Earl Friend is a heretic. He's a danger to the whole town."

"A danger, he is." Blackthorn gave Father Winthrop a condescending nod and looked at one of the armed men. "Find this Earl Friend. We'll see how soft he is."

"A soft-hearted woman," Winthrop added as the guard walked toward the steps. He turned to Muldoon. "You are a true citizen. I bow to your strength and courage."

Beck rolled his eyes. He hated the religious blather.

Blackthorn asked, "Fire or sword?"

"I'll burn, either way," Muldoon mumbled.

Father Winthrop crept to the edge of his seat. "Fire Cleanses the body and the soul only if the soul has not already fled the body."

Oh, please, thought Beck.

Muldoon shuffled nervously. Thick, glassy tears were in his eyes, though none rolled down his cheeks. "I...I don't think I can. I've heard the screams."

"Ecstasy," Winthrop said. He nodded several times to reinforce his argument. "That is simply the soul touching God."

Muldoon winced. "But it sounds like it hurts so much."

Beck felt sympathy for the man. "Take the sword. It'll end before you feel it. The fire will Cleanse you either way."

A flash of hope crossed Muldoon's face.

There was a shout and a scuffle from the back edge of the plaza. When Beck looked up, a dozen of Blackthorn's blue-shirted strongmen were wrangling a feisty Earl Friend toward the dais. Earl began to scream. He knew the fire was coming to lick his flesh. And like any sane man, he wanted no part of it.

Chapter 5: Ella

Ella stared down at the guards, then back up at her son. William had reached the top of the wall, and he swung his boot over the ledge, struggling to find footing.

"Keep going!" she screamed.

Hands tugged her from the wall, and a man's sweaty palm clamped her mouth. Her bag was ripped from her shoulder, and the contents spilled out over the grass. She attempted to fight, but the guard had a firm hold on her, and before she knew it, a knife poked against her abdomen.

She screamed uselessly into the hand on her mouth.

Her eyes flitted to William. He'd paused on the top of the ledge—just long enough to look back—and in that moment, she knew it was over.

"I got him!" the second guard yelled.

The guard leapt onto the wall; within seconds he'd made the climb. William swung his second leg over, but he was too late—the delay had cost him. The guard snagged onto his arm, and the boy cried out, pawing at the moss-covered stone.

"Do you want to fall, boy?"

As if to prove his point, the guard gave him a tug. William stopped squirming and looked down. He shook his head at the guard, tears welling in his eyes.

"Climb back down then. Slowly."

The boy complied, and the guard ushered him to the bottom. Ella tried to run to him, but the blade dug deeper into her side—a second warning. She replayed the last few minutes in her mind, trying to pinpoint the moment everything had dissolved.

She'd scouted the area before running to the wall. There'd been no sign of the guards. Had the men been hiding? Had they been waiting?

The second guard stared at her with a smug expression. She turned her head, catching a glimpse of the guard behind her.

Of course they'd known they were coming—maybe not Ella and William, perhaps, but someone. Although she didn't recognize the men, they looked about Ella's age. If she'd known about this section of the wall, then it was a safe bet they did, too.

She'd been stupid to come here.

Although she'd never been told the details of another's capture, she could assume they'd fallen into the same trap. No one had ever gotten away from town. At least that's what everybody said.

Why did she think she'd be any different?

She closed her eyes, trying to eliminate the false steps she'd taken. If she could do it over, she'd go toward the creek, or the river, or the mountains. There had to be places where the wall had crumbled.

Any border would've been better than here.

She was snapped to attention by rough hands on her dress. The first guard threw her to the ground, and the impact stung her knees. For the first time, she got a good look at the man that'd been holding her—gaunt cheeks, several day's stubble, and stained, smiling teeth.

"What're you fleeing for? You don't look infected."

Ella said nothing.

"She looks fine to me," the second guard said. "Better than fine, actually."

Ella glared at them, trying to regain her footing, but the second guard poked William with his knife. "Don't even try it," he said.

Ella dug her fingers into the ground, trying to control her emotions. First the Cleansings, then Ethan, and now this. How much could she take? How much could William?

"Mom?" William whimpered.

"It's okay, honey."

"No, it's not," the second guard said.

She gritted her teeth, trying to make her heart harden. Of all the bullshit and lies the Elders spread, maybe that was the one lesson worth learning.

How could someone hurt her, if she couldn't feel pain?

The first guard crouched next to her, spinning his knife in his hands. His eyes wandered from her face to her dress, and she could read his thoughts as if she'd had them herself.

These men had rules to follow, but what was stopping them from breaking those rules?

Who would believe a traitor's accusations?

Ella inched away from the men, trying to keep the attention on her. Trying to keep them away from William. The boy watched, and she could see the panic in his eyes.

"We're not infected," Ella pleaded.

"Then why are you running?" the first guard asked.

"We owe a debt to one of the merchants in town. He said he'd collect it after The Cleansing, and we don't have the money to pay him."

The guards were silent for a second. They exchanged glances.

It was a story that happened often, and one that rarely ended well. Usually the merchants would take out their debts in other ways—often by violence or sexual servitude, if the debtor were a woman of age—and the law allowed it.

"I'm telling the truth," Ella said. "You can Cleanse me, if you want—both of you. But afterward, you have to promise to let us go."

The guards looked at each other, as if they'd never heard the offer before. Ella couldn't imagine no one had ever attempted to bribe them. She'd heard the unclean ones say almost everything, when the pyre was lit and the guards were shuffling them toward the flames.

She moved her hand from the ground to her knee, purposely knocking away the ripped fold of her skirt, swallowing the sick feeling inside her.

The guard on the ground smirked, and his cheeks puffed in and out with excitement. "Okay," he said. He looked at the other guard, but the man had no objections.

The first guard moved toward her, relaxing his grip on the knife. William stared at them, his eyes wide.

"Wait," she said, holding up a finger.

"What is it?"

She pointed to a distant building, across the field. Then she let her eyes wander back to William. The guard nodded that he understood.

"Okay. Let's go."

The guard helped Ella to her feet, this time with a little more care, and she walked in front of him, still cognizant of the blade pressed against her back. The wind ruffled her skirt, and she held it in place, trying to preserve her last moments of dignity.

As they walked, she tried to envision a scenario that would interrupt the one she'd created. Maybe an unclean resident would run for the wall. Maybe another guard would take pity on them. Something. Anything.

The field before them was wide and vacant, and the buildings in the distance seemed as uninhabited as before. There was no sign of help. Anyone they ran into would probably make things worse—insisting they be taken to The Cleansing.

They'd probably be taken there anyway, once the guards were through.

All Ella had bought was time. Nothing more.

The knowledge hit her like a fist to the stomach, and suddenly she was crying, unable to hold back the tears.

"Keep moving," the guard behind her grunted, his courtesy waning.

She stifled her sobs, peering over her shoulder at William. The boy was following along, watching his feet. He was mumbling. She wondered if he knew what was coming.

Or was he having delusions again?

In some small way, she hoped that his head was somewhere else; that he'd be spared the memory of what was going to happen.

They left the shelter of the trees and entered the sunlit field. Ella tried to take in the moment, knowing the minutes to follow would be much worse. There were a lot of things that could be survived and forgotten, but this wouldn't be one of them. They reached the nearest building, and the knife receded from her back.

"Stay here, or we'll kill the boy," the guard said.

The guard walked out in front of her, peering into the decrepit building. The walls were filled with gaping holes, but the rooms were dark, and she could see little of the interior. A fitting place for such a vile act.

When he was satisfied the building was vacant, the guard looked at his friend.

"I'll go first," he said simply, as if they were setting up for a pig-pull, rather than stripping a woman of her decency.

The other guard nodded, and the first man pulled her into the building. She fought the urge to look back at her son. She couldn't meet William's eyes. Not now.

She stepped into the darkness, taking in the shapes and outlines of things she didn't recognize. Before she could make them out, the man grabbed hold of her arms. The stink of alcohol filled the air. She hadn't realized the guard was drunk before. Perhaps that was why he'd agreed to the proposal.

"Wait a second," she whispered, her pulse beating so fast she could barely think.

"What is it?"

He paused, his hands already pawing at her dress, his breath so bad she thought she'd vomit.

"Let me undo it. I don't want to rip the dress; it's the only one I have."

"Okay."

He let go of her, and suddenly she was free—mercifully free—if only for a few seconds. She searched for the buttons on her back, groping in the dark, feeling sick and nervous and angry. Her fingers trembled. She'd undressed a million times before, and now she could barely get her hands to cooperate.

It'd been over a year since she'd been with a man.

Of course, that was with Ethan.

But the guard in front of her wasn't a man, she reminded herself. He was a monster, as vile and corrupt as the others in town. The ones who'd burned her husband, and who'd burn her son, too, if she'd let them.

This was the last thing they'd take from her. She'd see to it.

She undid the top button, feeling the fabric loosen around her neck and shoulders. The man breathed harder. She reached up to shed the garment, crying as she smoothed out the ruffles. It was then that she heard the commotion from outside.

William shrieked.

She retracted her hands, starting for the door. Before she could proceed, the guard clamped his hand around her wrist and wrenched her backward.

"I don't think so." His voice was harsh and foul.

She tried pushing him away, but he stuck the knife back under her chin. A scream lodged in her throat, and her son's cries tore at her soul.

"You promised," she whispered.

"I promised nothing."

"You said that you'd let us go, once I was Cleansed."

Her eyes had adjusted, and she could make out the sneer on the man's face. She did her best to stay calm.

"No, I didn't."

"Please," she added. "Undress me, if you want. Just don't hurt my son."

She reached out for his arm, gently, pulling the man toward her. The man lowered his knife. He put his hands on her shoulders, resuming what he'd started. He slipped the top of the dress from her shoulders, and she felt it drop past her arms. She shuddered at the oily touch of his fingers.

Before he could get any further, Ella thrust her knee into the man's crotch.

The guard doubled over in pain, the breath hissing out of him. She heard a small thud in the dirt—the knife—and she dropped to the ground, searching for the handle. The guard was still bent over, trying to catch his breath. She patted the ground until her hands closed around the blade. Suddenly, the knife was in her hand, the man was grabbing her, and she was thrusting it into him.

The man let out a muted cry and fell back to the ground. Ella could feel his warm blood on her hand, but she didn't wait around to see what she'd done. Instead, she raced through the dark room and to the entrance, darting frantically for her son.

The daylight hit her—fast and sudden, blinding. She wiped her eyes. William was on the ground, partially disrobed. The second guard was standing over him, his blade held high in the air.

"He's infected!" he cried, as if the news would be a revelation to Ella.

Ella screamed and charged.

Before the guard could react, she barged into him with all the momentum of a mother's rage, knocking him backward to the ground. And then she was on top of him, heaving the knife into his chest, plunging it again and again, until the blade struck bone and the man was still.

She rolled off of him.

"Come on!" she screamed. Without looking back, Ella grabbed William's arm and ran for the nearby field, clutching her opened dress to her shoulders.

Chapter 6: Minister Beck

Beck stared across the dais at the condemned man, watching Muldoon's final moments. Muldoon stood naked from the waist up. Father Winthrop was inspecting him.

Careful not to touch Muldoon' skin, Winthrop's finger circled the smudge at the base of Muldoon's spine. "Come closer Franklin. Get a good look at this. This is classic smudge."

Franklin stepped forward. Before he could get a good look, Oliver poked out from behind him. "It looks like a bruise to me."

"Quiet, ignorant boy," Winthrop said, allowing his impatience with the boy to pull his temper to the surface.

Returning to his place at the back of the dais, Oliver muttered, "Looks like he got kicked by a horse."

Franklin turned to Oliver and shook his head. "Don't."

Muldoon remained tense, oblivious to the conversations going on around him.

Winthrop turned in his chair. "You must learn, boy. Tormenting this strong man with your childish speculations does him no favors. You watched your own father endure the flame. You should know."

"Yes, Father."

"You see, Franklin, the smudge is the size of a man's palm, and it usually appears here first. It has this bluish hue, sometimes with yellowed edges. Often, it appears on the elbows or knees, but occasionally it appears on the wrists or ankles."

"Why?" Franklin asked.

"The spore seeks the stony heart to bury its roots. But the spore is not wise. Any place where a man's bones are near the surface of the skin, the spore may settle."

"And the skull, too?" Franklin asked.

"Yes, especially the skull."

"Why not check there first?"

"Discolorations on the scalp are covered by the hair and near impossible to discern. We only find evidence on the skull after the spore has grown a wart."

"I understand."

"Muldoon," Father Winthrop waved his hand as if shooing a fly. "Show your smudge to General Blackthorn."

Muldoon shuffled to over in front of Blackthorn's chair, stopped and turned so that Blackthorn had a good view of his back.

"Indeed, a smudge," said General Blackthorn. "Show Minister Beck."

Muldoon shuffled.

Beck waited for Muldoon to stop and position himself.

The smudge looked like a bruise, indeed. Beck leaned close enough to smell the man's unwashed skin and whispered, "Take the sword, Muldoon."

Muldoon hesitated. "But I have a son."

"He will understand."

"He'll think that I am weak."

"Are you?" Beck sat back in his chair. "Turn and face me."

Muldoon obeyed. He held out his arms, palms up. "I have the strength of several men, when I am doing my work."

"Then your son will see that strength in you. You've already proven your bravery by standing in front of your fellows and showing your bru— smudge. Your son will know you are brave."

"May I ask a favor before I go to the pyre?"

Beck slumped in his chair. More than anything, he hated when they asked for favors. And it was always him they asked, never the others. On the rare days when a man came to the dais, pissing himself as he imagined the lick of flame on his skin, it was Winthrop who'd examine them first, always Winthrop, with his dim knowledge of anything beyond superstitions and stories. But he was the accepted expert in the ways the spore corrupted human flesh.

Expert my ass, Beck thought. That man wouldn't know a wart from a booger he'd dug out of his own nose.

After Winthrop, the unclean passed to Blackthorn who never dithered. He'd glance. He'd speak four or five syllables and wave them past. So it was inevitably Beck who got asked the favors—Beck, who had the misfortune of being the last kind face they'd each see before getting escorted to the pyre.

"My son has no one," Muldoon pleaded.

"You have no one at home?" Beck asked.

"No one. My wife was taken at the last Cleansing," Muldoon explained, pointing at the line of pyres. "She was the first of eighteen that day."

"I remember well," Beck said. "Your wife had the long raven hair."

Muldoon nodded. He squeezed his eyes shut, attempting to corral his tears.

Beck gave him a moment while he thought of the man's wife. She had been a gorgeous woman, just like the blonde girl who'd caught Beck's attention on the Cleansing platform earlier that day. Beck had been aroused by Muldoon's wife when she'd dropped her dress and walked up on the platform, looking down on the plaza with regal defiance. He'd often thought back to her naked body and perfect face when he was alone in his room at night.

But that had been a terrible day. They burned a dozen bodies and had to rebuild the pyres to burn six more. There were always stories from the past in which dozens, or even hundreds had been taken to the pyre. But the largest number any of the old men could remember seeing was the eighteen burned that day.

"She didn't scream," Muldoon finally said, breaking Beck's concentration.

"I remember." Beck nodded.

"If I cry out, when his mother did not, what will my son think of me?"

A commotion at the other end of the dais caught Beck's attention.

The armed men had stripped the heretic Earl Friend naked, and despite his frantic struggles, were dragging him onto the dais. If he'd been smudged before, it was impossible to tell: his body was speckled with welts and scrapes.

Seeing that his time had run out, Muldoon asked, "Will you take my son as an apprentice?"

Back to this, Beck thought with annoyance. It was hard for him to hide his disinterest. Still, he had to say something to the man. "The orphanage takes excellent care of our parentless children. It assists them in an apprenticeship when they are of the age."

Muldoon looked at the ground. "He's too old for the orphanage."

"Then he is too old to apprentice for me. Scholars must be taught from a young age."

"Yes. I understand that. I just—"

"Why is he not a rabbit hunter? Why did you not teach him your trade?"

"He hunts. But he's different."

Beck was losing his patience. "Children, even ones who would prefer not to be taught the joy of hard labor, must be taught by their parents. Perhaps you have been too indulgent with the boy."

Muldoon fell to his knees. "Please, please. I beg of you. Speak to him. You'll see."

"What will I see? An insolent boy? A lazy boy who disrespects his father?" Beck's voice was as harsh as the insult. He had to remind himself that it was wrong to be cruel to a man on his way to the pyre. With an effort, he softened the angry scowl on his face and gave Muldoon a look that let him know he could speak again, if he wished.

"He reads."

Beck was taken aback. That couldn't be possible. "How did that come to pass?"

Muldoon hesitated as though hiding something. "I've seen him."

"Seen him read?"

"Yes."

"And who taught him? Do you read, Muldoon?"

"No, Minister Beck. I do not."

"Yet you believe that your son reads?"

"I've seen him with books."

"Books? You have books? Are you rich?"

Muldoon shook his head and stared at the ground. Two armed men had come to stand beside him. One said, "It's time, Minister Beck."

"Stand," the other one barked at Muldoon.

Beck raised a hand to delay them. "And where did you get books?"

Muldoon looked around, as though preparing to share a secret. In a soft voice he said, "He found them."

"Found them?" Beck furrowed his brow. "A book hasn't been found in nearly two hundred years. Did this boy steal these books?"

"No, no. I swear he did not steal them."

"Are you sure? If you are sending me off to chase a lie, nothing more can be done to you, of course, but I assure you, Muldoon, your lie will not go easy on this boy. Does he have these books?"

"He really has them."

A guard spoke. "Minister Beck." It was time for Muldoon to go.

"Please," Muldoon begged.

Just to satisfy the man, Beck said. "I will visit your son. I will see if he has these books. And I'll consider him for scholarship." It all felt like lies. But then, it was. Sure, if the kid had books, if he could read, then yes, he could be considered for scholarship, but that was unlikely. If the boy had happened upon an ancient cache of books—or even a few—mysteriously preserved by time, he might open the pages and pretend to read. That might be the truth of it. The second truth was that the boy could not appreciate the great value of old books, not like Beck could. The books should be taken from the boy, lest he ruin them.

Of course, that lie Beck told himself didn't mention the great value of the old books.

"Thank you, Minister Beck. Thank you. His name is Ivory. You'll find him at the first house past the big barn at the end of the Hay Road, where the fields begin. Thank you so much."

Beck smiled weakly as the armed men took Muldoon away.

Chapter 7: Muldoon

Muldoon's heart hammered as he steeled himself for the end.

The women sang the Fire Dirge, while the men swayed slowly with the rhythm. Clouds blew across the sky, collecting for a storm, stiffening the wind.

Muldoon stood atop a pile of logs, branches, and kindling twigs stacked five feet deep. His hands were bound behind him, around the pyre pole. On the pole to Muldoon's left, Earl Friend spat curses at Muldoon. Earl was going to God as a coward, shaming his wife and kids in front of every solemn face in the plaza.

To Earl's left, three women were bound atop their own pyres, waiting for the fire to Cleanse their smudged and warty skin. Two of those women sobbed, but everyone expected that of women. A gravelly voiced woman called Margaret the Wench strained against her pole pleading to the people, pleading to the three silent Elders on the dais, pleading to the clouds and the heavens.

"Mercy. Save me. Give me the sword. I beg you." Unfortunately Margaret was wasting her words on the ears of people who mostly despised her. She would soon be touched by fire. She would not get the mercy of the blade. Everybody knew that.

Women always hid their shameful uncleanliness until it was revealed on the Cleansing platform, in front of all. In choosing to hide, women lost their right to the sword, just as Earl Friend had lost his. The sword could only be chosen by someone brave enough to come forward of his own accord, as Muldoon had done. Absent that choice, fire was the only other passage to God.

Muldoon had chosen the fire over the blade.

The dirge drew to its end. The women started it again, anticipating the first fire, the one to be lit under Muldoon's feet. When that happened, the women would sing louder to cover his screams. They would sing louder to wail their pain and fright. They would sing until blackened bones hung from the pyre poles and only smoking ash remained below.

After, they would go to their houses, thank the gods for their cleanliness, and prepare a simple meal for the men, who had to bear the shame of the day on their faces. The men always had shame on their faces, a shame that was never vocalized, nor explained. Those meals were silent. And silence followed the townsfolk to bed, where husbands would hold their wives close, thanking their god for their luck.

Chapter 8: Oliver

Oliver was tired of standing. He was tired of looking at the faces of so many sad women. He hated the fire dirge and he hated Cleansing Day. It was a Cleansing Day that took both his parents and left him apprenticed to Father Winthrop; Winthrop was a buffoon at best, a simple-minded bully at worst.

At first, Oliver was thankful. An apprenticeship in the clergy left him regularly fed, and at least standing on the fringes of luxury, such at it was. The alternative was the orphanage, home of empty stomachs and cold nights that only served to funnel ignorant boys into a life of hard labor in the fields. Even as young as Oliver was, he knew he didn't want that.

What Oliver wanted was anything that would take him outside the walls. He wanted to see the ancient ruined cities and explore the ancients' ways. He wanted to learn their secrets. He dreamt about life as one of Beck's Scholars and hated memorizing Father Winthrop's endless litany of contradictory parables.

Or a soldier. Oliver flexed his spindly arms and imagined himself on a horse, sword in hand, charging a horde of reeking demons, hacking off their bulbous, deformed heads, saving weak villagers and their children.

Yes, Oliver could be a hero.

That would be a life.

The sound of the dirge got louder, interrupting Oliver's daydreams, drawing his gaze back to the row of pyres. The torch had just touched the kindling below Muldoon's feet.

The screams were coming.

Oliver wanted to cover his ears, as he used to do when hiding among the skirts of the women in the plaza. But he was just a little kid then. Up on the dais, Father Winthrop forbade such behavior explicitly. To show anything but a brave face in front of the women was to invite the switch or the belt. Such was the price of life in the clergy.

Father Winthrop told him that the chosen were stronger, wiser, and kinder then regular men.

Kinder?

Oliver nearly laughed at the irony of it. Could anyone as unkind as Winthrop, as unable to see it in himself, still be wise? No.

The crackle of burning logs cut through the baleful dirge.

Oliver looked at his feet and started to hum quietly along, hoping the sound in his head might keep the screams out of his ears.

Franklin elbowed Oliver and turned on him with furrowed brows.

Oliver understood the look, stopped humming, and turned his face toward Muldoon. He tried vainly to focus on the gray clouds out on the horizon.

The orange flames touched Muldoon's pants and they started to smoke.

That would only last for a few seconds. Oliver had seen it too many times before. Men's silence rarely lasted past the time when the pants started to blaze. The fire wasn't yet hot enough to kill, but was hot enough to crisp their skin.

And the pants blazed.

Muldoon's face stretched a silent grimace, split open at the mouth, wider and wider in a pantomime of a writhing scream.

Then his voice, unable to dam agony, pierced air.

In a voice probably meant to be heard only in his head, Father Winthrop said, "The ecstasy."

Oliver hated him for that.

Chapter 9: Ella

Ella and William kept running long after the wall had disappeared and the trees had grown thick around them. Even though they'd fled the town, she could still hear the gurgle of the first guard's cries, and she could envision the knife sticking from the second guard's stomach like a misplaced limb.

Her hands were wet with crimson, but she didn't dare stop to wipe them off. Instead, she let the blood dry in the wind as she ran. Her dress was equally stained.

She'd wash the blood later, in a brook or a stream or the Davenport River, whatever body of water she came across first. One step at a time, Ella. Right now her main goal was to distance herself from a place she no longer wanted to call home.

"Are you all right, William?"

In her haste to get over the wall, she'd barely had a chance to check on him. The boy nodded, his eyes still wide with fear, his clothes disheveled and hanging off him. They'd both been degraded. But it could've been worse.

Far, far, worse.

There was a chance it would get worse, if she didn't get them away from the wall as quickly as possible. The guards would be looking for them soon. Two of them were dead, but there'd be others. And the disrespect she'd felt at their hands would be nothing compared to what was coming.

The pyre. The spike. A hanging. She didn't know which she'd receive, or which was worse.

In her weakest moments, she'd often longed for one of those fates, back in the days when Ethan had first passed. But those days seemed so long ago. Her duty now was to protect William, and she had an obligation to get him away from the town and away from the slaughter. Free from the downturned glances of unhappy women and the lustful eyes of men.

They needed to forge a new life.

They'd been running for ten minutes when William's hand slipped from hers. He bent over, clutching his side, breathing fast and erratic.

"Are you okay?"

"I need to rest, Mom," he managed, between breaths.

She felt a sting of mother's guilt, and she bent down and put her hands on the boy's shoulders, subconsciously wondering if she'd find something other than thin bones.

"It'll be all right, William. We'll rest for a moment, but then we have to keep going."

She put her ear to the wind, sure she'd hear the distant cries of men, but all she heard for certain was the rustle of the trees and the occasional chatter of an animal. She realized she had no idea what was lurking in these woods.

It'd been twelve years since she'd been outside of the town's dilapidated wall.

The last time she'd been in the wild was when she'd traveled from Davenport to Brighton, preparing to become Ethan's wife.

And now she was going to make that return journey with her own son, hoping to reunite with her aunt and uncle — the relatives who'd raised her — and take refuge. Her aunt and uncle had visited her several times in Brighton, but she'd never returned to visit them. It was a risky proposition, but one at which she knew she couldn't fail. To stop would be to surrender herself and her son to the hands of the townspeople.

She couldn't do that.

"Are you ready?" she asked.

The boy nodded. She grabbed William's hand again, her hands still slippery with the guard's blood. She noticed his shirt was stretched and sagging, and she pulled it over his neck, covering the lump that had exposed itself to the sun.

His sin had become hers.

She'd get them out of this, even if it was the last thing she did.

***

They ran until Ella was stiff and sore and having trouble breathing. The stitches in her side threatened to keel her over. She imagined her son felt even worse. Although he was younger and more used to the exercise, his legs were shorter.

They'd been alternating speeds since they left—changing from a sprint to a jog and back again. Every time she heard a noise in the forest, Ella would panic and pull her son faster. When they'd gotten clear of the disturbance, they'd slow down again. It was an exhausting game of nerves versus energy, one from which she needed a break.

For several minutes, they'd heard the sound of water, and Ella had been trying to track down the source. Now she could see it in the distance—a clear, bubbling river that was almost the width of her house.

She recognized it immediately. Davenport River. She'd been by it with Ethan and the guide twelve years ago. The road to Davenport couldn't be far.

William stared, his eyes tracing the swift current. They'd both been to the River of Brighton plenty of times, but he'd never been to this one. Ella was always amazed at the power of flowing water, the way it twisted and furled over the stones and sunken trees beneath it, finding its way through.

She allowed her gaze to wander for a few seconds before she bent down and crept to the edge. The river foamed and spat.

"Stay back," she warned.

She dipped her hands in the water, letting the cold soak her skin, and then scrubbed her hands together. She could still smell the odor of the guard's blood, and she held her breath as it washed away. Her dress was red and blemished. In her efforts to hold it up, she'd stained both the collar and the shoulders. She'd have to clean it before they ran into someone.

When she looked back, William was staring at his own grime-covered hands.

"Come here," she urged.

The boy obeyed and scooted next to her. She helped him rinse off. Thankfully, his shirt was unscathed, although it'd been stretched out from where the guard had yanked it. She fixed him as best she could and then sent him back a few feet.

She scanned the banks of the river on either side, searching for danger, but saw nothing. As much as she hated to slow down, she knew that she'd need to clean her clothing to avoid suspicion.

"Can you look away for a moment, honey?" she asked William.

The boy obliged. Ella glanced around the forest, unbuttoned her dress, and slipped it over her head. The breeze was cool against her skin. It caressed her shoulders and tickled the inside of her arms. Being exposed in the woods felt strange and uncomfortable, but it was still better than being exposed on the Cleansing platform.

Anything was better than that.

She knelt down on the riverbed and began scrubbing at the top of her dress. To her relief, she was able to get off some of the blood, but some of it remained, and she did her best to dilute it. If someone inquired as to its origin, she'd blame it on a food spill, or perhaps a wound from a sewing needle.

When she'd cleaned the garment, she shook it out to dry it a bit, and slipped it back over her head.

It was the best she could do.

When she glanced back at William, he was still staring at the river. She walked up the bank to meet him.

"'I'm all set, sweetie. We can go now."

The boy was holding their bags. She took one of them from his grasp and hefted it over her shoulder.

"Put yours on," she said.

She was about to slip hers on when she noticed the boy wasn't moving.

"Are they dead?" he asked. "The guards?"

"I think so." She set her bag down and leaned next to him. "They were going to hurt us, William."

"I know that."

She studied his eyes, trying to see what was lurking behind them. As much as she'd tried to protect him, he'd seen as much bloodshed as she. The pyres. The spikes. Ethan burning. It'd been six months since he'd had a nightmare, but she still worried about him. How could any boy be expected to forget all that?

The children were exposed to the same things the adults were. There was a time when Father Winthrop enforced protection for the younger ones, but those days were long gone. Ella didn't believe that was fair, or just. But what could she do?

The worst part of her job as a parent was the explanations. As much as it pained her, sometimes there just weren't any good answers.

William still wasn't moving. She stroked his hair and stared at the river with him.

She'd been ready to go for almost a minute, but she could sense that he needed another. After a few seconds, he looked at her.

"Am I going to die, Mom?"

Ella choked on her answer before she said it. "Of course not."

William's hands moved to his neck, and she fought the urge to pull them off. Not here, not now, she wanted to scream. Instead she kept quiet. The boy rubbed the back of his neck, as if a gnat had bitten him, and then placed his hands back at his sides.

"Will I feel it when it happens? Will I feel it when I turn?"

Ella shook her head. In truth, she had no idea. Didn't want to think about it. They had plenty of time left, plenty of time to build a new life…She wasn't ready to handle this…not now…not yet.

"No," she forced herself to say. "I don't think so."

William nodded, his face grim and composed, looking much too mature for a boy his age. She stroked his hair one last time and then got to her feet, slinging her bag on her shoulder.

"We have to leave."

"I know," he said. "We're going to Davenport, right? To see Aunt Jean and Uncle Frederick?"

"Yes."

"Is it nice there?"

"It's beautiful. Probably the most beautiful village I've ever seen," Ella said.

A smile flitted across William's face as he tugged his pack onto his shoulder. He reached out and took her hand, breaking his trance from the river.

Chapter 10: General Blackthorn

Blackthorn listened to the fire dirge and thought about all the places he'd rather be than sitting in his chair, watching the lucky thousands wail their fright, as though death had come to them personally. Fear was an insidious, contagious thing.

First, those nearest the flames reacted, as though they held some hope that the ritual would not be carried through to its ashen end, that the flame would not burn, that the torch would not be laid at the foot of the pyre. But of course it would; a tiny fiery star, a pinprick of horror.

He watched that dread ripple through the crowd faster than the flames surged through the dry wood. Women swooned and children trembled, each catching the emotion from the person in front of him or her, fear manifesting itself in a visible wave that rolled over the mass of the weak-hearted.

Maybe that's what Blackthorn disliked most about Cleansing Day. Fear became real. He saw it. He smelled it. He tasted it in the air. It reminded him of cloying, urine soaked britches, and the wet bed sheets of a boy too afraid to go to the outhouse in the dark of night. It brought back memories of the worst days of his life, when panic ruled him as a boy, leading up to that moment when his father, the great man, fell from his horse and was swarmed by the beasts.

Emotion welled up in his hard heart. He gritted his teeth, sucked in his breath, and recalled how the fear had transformed him from weak boy into the stone-hard man that he now was, Supreme Leader of all in the three towns and every village in between. Sure, there were Beck and

Winthrop, the other two in the Council of Elders, but they were weak. They were figureheads pretending to be leaders.

Movement to his right distracted Blackthorn from his thoughts.

Three of Beck's census men were in front of Beck, showing him their lists, reviewing their calculations with anxious gestures and quivering voices. Blackthorn didn't need to hear their words to know that the numbers didn't add up. For the census takers, men who sat in the night squinting at papers on candlelit tables—men who would never raise a sword in anger, or have the blood of a brother on their hands—this was the pinnacle of fear.

Blackthorn hated them, necessary though they were.

The weak, hunchbacked writers of numbers performed an important duty. In taking the Cleansing census, they also wrote down the names of any missing women, the ones too afraid to face the pyre.

The fact that there were still runners sickened Blackthorn. Unfortunately, the Muldoons of the world were becoming a rarer and rarer occurrence. With each Cleansing that passed, fear had taken root and was growing. Deceitful behavior was becoming the norm. Frightened people were too weak of heart to walk the road to courage without a little helpful prodding.

The census men finished their presentation, and Beck made some disappointed sounds. He motioned for the men to present the results to Blackthorn. Blackthorn didn't need to be told. Nevertheless, he let them approach. The ritual was a necessary one. Structure helped simple-minded men manage the anxieties in their lives. Brighton had more than its share of simple-minded men.

Beck's three census men lined up, shoulder to shoulder in front of Blackthorn. The one in the middle, a chinless man with darting eyes, said, "General Blackthorn, we have the results of the Cleansing census."

"Speak."

It was the chinless man's first time to present the numbers, and he was troubled. Blackthorn half expected to see a puddle form at the man's feet. He even wagered to himself on which would come first—the urine or the man's words.

To his surprise, the words won. The census man said, "There are two missing from the count."

Blackthorn nodded sternly. There was no need to feign surprise. No need for anger. Solutions were necessary.

Looking around again, the chinless man's eyes fell to Beck, searching for direction.

Beck waved his hand in small circles. "Speak, man."

The chinless man looked back at Blackthorn. His eyes slowly sank from Blackthorn's face to his feet. "Ella Barrow and her son William are not present, General."

Blackthorn nodded to his left, gesturing a direction for the three census men to take. "Go," he told them.

Two soldiers came to fill the space in front of Blackthorn, and all on the dais waited while Blackthorn contemplated his words. He let the tension build, even though there was no decision to be made. Ella and William would be found. They would be brought to the square, flailed for their cowardice, and placed atop particularly slow smoldering pyres that would lick their flesh clean for many long, agonizing minutes.

Then their souls would be taken to God.

"Captain Swan," Blackthorn said.

Captain Swan, one of the two standing in front of Blackthorn said, "Yes, General."

"Send troops to find this woman Ella and her son. Bring her back to the square."

"Yes, General." Captain Swan and the captain beside him turned crisply, stepping toward the stairs.

"Captain Townshend."

The second captain came to a halt. Captain Swan stopped alongside him.

"Captain Swan, you have your task. Go." Blackthorn stood, surprising everyone on the dais with the divergence from protocol. Normally the two captains would go off together. "Captain Townshend, you have another task."

"Yes, General."

General Blackthorn walked to the front edge of the dais.

Just as the fear had rippled across the women when the pyres were lit, a new ripple spread out from the crowd, emanating from Blackthorn himself as though he were the hottest flame they'd seen, hot enough to burn them all. No word could be heard, not a cough or a sneeze.

Blackthorn said, "Two of the unclean have chosen weakness over strength, fear over courage." He paused, letting the gravity the betrayal sink in. It wasn't a betrayal of Blackthorn, or the Council of Elders—it was a betrayal of Brighton.

"Fear is growing among us. Dread makes our hearts soft. It destroys our unity, and weakens the three towns. Fear is infectious. Left unchecked, it will destroy the efforts of the strong. It will destroy what our fathers have built. It will destroy us all."

He paused again, for effect.

"All who support weakness and fear must meet the pyre." Blackthorn cast his glare slowly across the women. "These two runners did not act alone. Nobody turns unclean and runs without those around him knowing. And when we, the people of Brighton, do nothing to Cleanse this fear, the spore takes root and we are all guilty. In this case, the family, the neighbors, and the close friends of Ella Barrow and her boy William are complicit."

Gasps rippled through the crowd.

"Captain Townshend, bring before us this woman's family. Bring her neighbors. Bring her friends. We will sort this out, and the pyre will mete our town's justice and Cleanse them."

Stifled cries emanated from the crowd, and heads drooped. Hands covered mouths to whisper protests.

Minister Beck stepped up out of his chair. "General Blackthorn, this is not a decision to be taken by one Elder alone."

Without turning, Blackthorn asked, "Father Winthrop, do you concur?"

Put on the spot, Father Winthrop gasped. He rubbed a shaking hand over his chin and glanced at Minister Beck, but turned away before he caught Beck's eye. Weakly, Winthrop murmured, "Ah…um… Yes. I… concur."

Beck flushed red with rage.

Keeping a repressive eye on the women in the square and the men on the fringe, Blackthorn said, "Captain Townshend, bring us all of Ella Barrow's accomplices."

Chapter 11: Ella

Ella recognized the road to Davenport immediately.

Davenport Road was little more than a ten-foot wide trail, worn down by years of foot and hoof. At one point, the road crossed a great field and branched off to Coventry, but mostly it ran close to the river.

Everyone knew if you followed the river, you'd eventually get to Davenport. But the river snaked a circuitous path. If followed exactly, it would lead a traveler through the forests for days and days. There were many paths that branched to smaller villages, and without the services of a guide, a traveller from Brighton might end up in any of a dozen places.

Getting lost was the least of Ella's worries. Getting caught was her major concern. If the Elders sent the guards to look for her and William, they'd follow the roads out of Brighton. Her and William needed to avoid the roads.

The river was their best bet.

As simple as the idea was, following the river was more of a challenge than Ella had hoped. In several places, the ground was too rough or steep, or the forest was too dense to navigate. Creeks ran into the river and cut right across their path, sometimes flowing through ravines so deep they couldn't be crossed. There were the spots where Ella and William would come to a hard curve in the river, watching it flow off to their right. Rather than follow it, they'd tromp through the woods, following the sound of the strong current somewhere off in the trees, trying to shave a mile or two off their journey.

It was on one such tromp that they lost sight of the river and ran across a long, perfectly straight wall, made from what appeared to be a single piece of waist-high stone.

"Ancient Stone," Ella said as she laid a hand on the wall, showing it to William. He was already preoccupied with another wall, running parallel to the first but five feet above, across a gap. Above that was another, and another, alternating bands of ancient stone and gaps that grew thick with shrubs and vines. The layers stacked up into the air on thick square posts until they stopped just above the tallest trees.

"What is it?" asked William.

Shaking her head, Ella said, "I don't know."

"Did the Ancients live here?"

It didn't look like a house or anything she'd seen back in Brighton. And it didn't look like anything she'd seen in Davenport, either. At least, not that she remembered. All the ancient buildings there looked like they'd once served a purpose. Some had rooms that looked like they could have been sleeping quarters, or possible merchants stores. Some could have been storehouses.

But the function of this giant, cubed-shaped thing was lost on her.

Between the bushes that jutted out between the layers, she could see murky, empty shadows and far through the other side she saw the outlines of tree trunks in the sunshine. The inside appeared to be a quarter the size of the square in Brighton. Why would the Ancients have constructed such thing?

"I'll bet we're the first people in a thousand years to be here," William said in awe.

"Maybe," Ella responded. She looked around, as if the guards might've already caught up to them. Despite her concern, she knew it was getting late; they'd been traveling for the greater part of a day, and soon they'd need to take shelter for the night. The boy's words finally hit her. "A thousand years?" She looked down at William and smiled. "You don't even know what a thousand years is, you silly boy."

"I do," William said confidently. "You don't, but I do."

Shaking her head, Ella motioned William to follow her. She started walking the length of the wall, looking inside between the shrubs and admiring the towering layers of Ancient Stone. "You're right. I don't know what a thousand is. My uncle Frederick taught me to count to a hundred when I was your age. A hundred was all I ever needed. I seldom need to count anything more than a dozen."

William brushed his fingers along the ancient wall as they walked. "A thousand is easy. It's just like counting to a hundred ten times. That's all."

"And how would you know that?" Ella asked, not believing a word of it, but happy for a moment to forget their troubles and have a normal conversation.

"When we're at the market, I heard merchants talking about numbers, some big, some small, adding them up and subtracting them even."

"Adding and subtracting?" Ella laughed. "You're going to tell me now that you can add and subtract and you learned it listening to merchants talk?"

"Yes," William's tone was completely serious.

Ella stopped, turned and knelt down in front of William. It wasn't until she'd assumed the position that she realized he was too tall. On her knees, she had to look up at him. "You're growing up too fast, William. You're going to be as big as your father."

"I know."

Ella stood. "You know, merchants hire tutors to teach their kids numbers and how to add and subtract."

William shrugged. "Why do they need tutors? It's not that hard."

"I'll take your word for it." Ella turned and started back along the wall. "I can add a few numbers, but I can't subtract them."

"It's just like adding, only backwards."

"If you say so."

William stopped. "We can climb over if you want."

Ella looked around at the forest and back up at the layered walls. "I know."

"What are we waiting for, then?" asked William.

"I'm not sure." She sniffed the air.

William copied her and sniffed the air too.

Ella pushed her head between some shrubs, trying to get a whiff inside the ancient structure.

"What are we trying to smell?" William asked.

Ella pulled her head out of the bushes and looked down at her son, not wanting to scare him further.

"Demons?" William guessed.

"How could you know that?"

"My friend Mickey said they stink. He said they smell worse than pigs."

Ella nodded. She'd heard the same.

William jumped up, leaning over the wall and through the vegetation, sniffing inside. "I don't smell anything bad in here." He slid back off. "Do you think its safe?"

"I don't know."

"Do you think the demons will catch us if we go inside?"

"Don't speak of such things," Ella said, though the same fear lurked inside her.

Unfazed, William continued, "Everybody knows they're out here, mom. I'm not a little kid anymore."

"Yes you are," Ella said. "You just think because you know what a thousand is that you're suddenly a grown-up?"

William made a show of looking up and down the length of the building and up to its tallest wall. "I think we should stay here tonight. It'll be dark before you think."

The boy was right.

"Okay," Ella conceded. "We'll go inside and see. But stay quiet and stay close. Do you hear me?"

***

The structure was a strange, strange place indeed.

Once inside the layered building, Ella and William found themselves on a gently sloping floor that spiraled up and up. They realized very quickly that they were on the second, then the third floor. When they came out on the top, the structure opened up to sunshine and a perfectly square meadow with a few small trees, wild flowers, and clumps of blueberry bushes surrounded by a waist-high wall of ancient stone.

The first thing William did was run to the edge and look out across the tops of trees, which surrounded the old building. Ella followed at a walking pace, scanning the meadow for any hazards. When she reached the edge, she took up next to William and placed her hands on the wall.

Far out toward the direction of the mountains, she saw a trail of black smoke drifting up into the wind. It didn't take a lot of imagination to guess what that was. The pyres of Brighton. She gulped as she scanned the horizon. Way off to the south, she thought she could make out another smudge of black on the late afternoon blue sky. Could those be the Coventry pyres? All three towns and the major villages

Cleansed on the same day. That was an unbreakable tradition.

William's voice distracted her. "I like it up here."

"Me too, honey."

"You can see forever."

"A thousand miles." Ella smiled and nudged William. She didn't even know for sure what a mile looked like, just that it was a long way.

"Maybe a thousand miles." William shrugged. He pointed at the mountains far in the east. "How far are away are they?"

"I don't know," Ella said. "I've never been, and I don't know anyone who has."

"I'd like to climb them some day. I'll bet if you climbed up one of those mountains you could see the whole world."

"Maybe."

Ella and William watched the distant mountains. After a while, he asked, in a serious voice, "Did we run away from Brighton?"

"Yes."

"Are we going back?"

"No." Ella kept her eyes on the horizon.

William said, "We could stay here and live. I like this place. I could be king of the ancient box building." He smiled and turned, taking off at a serpentine run. "King William. King William."

Ella turned and followed. She veered close to one of the clumps of blueberry bushes and was pleased to see they were covered with berries. She called to William, "Remember what I told you."

William spun around in circles. "I remember everything," he called.

"Look for big tracks and look for scat. Bears like berries as much as we do."

"I looked already." William took off at a sprint to another side of the meadow. "Nothing's up here but us."

Ella looked out across the meadow again. Any animal big enough to hurt her or William would be visible, unless it crouched in the blueberry bushes. She hoped. She walked slowly, looking for signs of animals, but all she found were tiny round pellets of rabbit dung.

If only she knew how to hunt those quick little tasty rodents.

***

With William's help, Ella found enough long branches to lean against one of the walls in a corner of the meadow. Beneath that crude shelter they laid their blankets. When the last of the sun's light faded from the evening sky, they'd have a place to cover themselves. Their bellies were full of blueberries. Their flasks were getting low on water, but they'd find their way back to the river in the morning.

Despite how the day had started, Ella felt good about their situation. They'd escaped The Cleansing. William was acting precocious and energetic, as always. And they hadn't seen a single pursuer.

Perhaps they'd already escaped.

"Mom, what do you think happened to the Ancients?"

"I don't know, honey. Nobody does."

"There are stories, right?"

Ella leaned up on an elbow to look at William. "People say the twisted men killed them. Some legends say the Ancients turned into the twisted men."

"The demons are the Ancients? Do you think that's so?"

"That isn't the kind of question that little boys should spend their time thinking about."

"I'm curious, though, Mom. Tell me what you think."

"I'm not sure, William. I heard Father Winthrop talk about it once at the devotional service."

"What did he say?"

Ella laughed and thought about it. "I honestly don't know. He's full of more meaningless words than any man I've ever met."

They both laughed. After a moment, William's face turned serious. "Dad used to tell me that I'd understand when I got older. He told me that in time, The Word would become clear."

Ella leaned in close and whispered. "I've got a secret to tell you."

"What's that?"

"That's just something parents tell their kids when they don't have the answer. Don't tell any of the other kids, okay?"

William laughed, and so did Ella. Soon they were asleep.

Chapter 12: Oliver

Oliver stood beside Franklin, watching the morning bustle. The people on Market Street went about their business as they always did, but the energy had drained out of them. There were few jokes and few smiles. Conversation was hushed. It wasn't unusual for the mood in the market to be a little off the day after The Cleansing, but this morning's gloom made Oliver stay close to Franklin's side. The mood frightened him in a way he couldn't define.

Pointing at a stall of vegetables, Franklin said, "Usually at this time of morning there's plenty to choose from. I wonder if all the women shopped early today."

Oliver looked around, afraid his voice might carry. "I think people are afraid of what General Blackthorn is going to do with Ella Barrow's friends."

Franklin rolled his eyes. "That's got nothing to do with a food shortage in the market."

Oliver punched Franklin in the arm, hard enough to show his displeasure. "Father Winthrop treats me like I'm stupid all day long. Don't you start."

Franklin turned to Oliver, started to say something and stopped. He took a deep breath and said, "Father Winthrop talks to you like you're stupid because you won't stop playing that game with him."

Oliver looked innocently at Franklin. "What game?"

Franklin pushed Oliver, turned, and started up the street. "That game. You act like you're a naïve, ignorant peasant and everybody believes it because you're just a little kid. But every time you do it, you start asking Father Winthrop questions and at the end of it, he starts to feel stupid and loses his temper. That's why he talks to you like your stupid. Because you make him feel stupid."

Oliver shrugged. "He beats me with a switch. He deserves it."

"Because you make him feel stupid. Just—" Franklin gave up on what he was going to say. "Don't worry about it. Do what you want to do. Maybe you like getting beaten."

Oliver shook his head. He didn't like it one bit. Under his breath he said, "I hate him."

Franklin spun on Oliver and leaned over. "Don't ever say that out loud again. You hear me?"

Oliver nodded.

"He'll beat you and put you in the orphanage or he'll see a smudge on you—"

"I don't have a smudge," Oliver said, suddenly frantic.

"That's what you don't understand, Oliver. It doesn't have to be there. Men with angry eyes see what they want to see. If you make him angry enough, he'll see a smudge and he'll put you on the pyre."

"The pyre?" Oliver's mouth hung open.

Franklin's face softened and he straightened up. "Don't you start crying. Not here. Not in the market." Franklin looked around.

Oliver cleared his throat and stood as straight as he could. "Sorry."

"Men don't cry. You know that."

Oliver nodded. Everybody knew that.

Franklin put an arm over Oliver's shoulder and pulled him along. "Come on. We need a rabbit. Father Nelson is on his way from Coventry. He'll be here for lunch and Father Winthrop wants Rabbit Stew."

Oliver sniffled and rubbed his eyes. "How did Father Nelson get here from Coventry so fast? What about The Cleansing there?"

"They moved Novice Willard up to Father Willard," Franklin said.

"Willard is an imbecile." Oliver spat on the ground.

Franklin shook his head. "Father Willard took Father Nelson's place in presiding over The Cleansing in Coventry."

Oliver asked, "What's Father Nelson doing here?"

"I don't know." Franklin said, "I want to help you, Oliver. You know that right?"

"I know. You're my only friend, Franklin."

Franklin nodded, gave Oliver a squeeze and let him go. "If you have questions, ask me, okay? Just do what Father Winthrop says, smile, and get good at keeping your mouth shut."

"But there are so many things I don't understand." Oliver planted his feet. He pointed back in the direction of the church building where Father Winthrop was probably still lying lazily in his giant bed, scratching himself and farting. "He knows The Word. He says The Word has all the answers but he never answers me."

Franklin shushed Oliver. "That's what I mean. You need to learn not to say those things."

"I can't ask questions?"

Franklin leaned in close and in a whisper said, "Don't ever question The Word. Ever. I don't care if you believe it or not. You learn it when Father Winthrop teaches you. But you don't ever, ever question it. If you think Father Winthrop's beatings are bad now, wait until he hears you say something like that."

Oliver looked at his feet. "Sorry."

Franklin straightened and pointed to an empty place on the street. "Muldoon used to set up his stall there."

Oliver looked over. "He won't be bringing anymore rabbits, I guess."

"I guess not." Franklin started up the street again. "As I was saying, you can ask me anything. I might not have the answers, but Scholar Evan is a friend of mine, and he knows things most people don't. Beck's scholars have a collection of ancient books—nearly twenty of them."

Oliver's eyes went wide. "They're rich?"

Franklin nodded. "But they don't see it that way. They study the books trying to learn about the past."

"What do they learn?" Oliver asked.

"I don't know. I'll ask Evan about it next time I see him."

Oliver walked along beside Franklin for a moment, trying to think of all the questions that nagged him, but his mind was suddenly blank.

Franklin walked up to a stall where a vendor had five rabbits hanging by their feet. "I need a fat one," he told the vendor. "A fresh one. It's for Father Winthrop."

Oliver looked at the vendor's face as Franklin said it. The vendor's face flashed resentment, then stretched into a fawning, artificial smile.

The vendor looked at the rabbits he had hanging by their hind feet. Then he glanced down at a covered basket by his own feet.

"The rabbit?" Franklin said with a frown.

The vendor seemed to deflate. "Of course." He knelt down, flipped back the cloth that had been covering a basket, and exposed a rabbit that hadn't yet been hung. "I killed this fat one before dawn. Father Winthrop will like it more than these others." He pointed at the hanging rabbits. "These aren't as fresh."

He extended the rabbit, and Oliver reached up and accepted it. As the younger novice, it was his duty to carry it for Franklin.

"My compliments," said the Vendor.

Of course, thought Oliver. That's what they all said. The clergy ate for free. It was the duty of any farmer or hunter to provide food upon request.

Franklin said, "Father Winthrop thanks you for strengthening The Word through your efforts."

With that, the transaction ended and the two walked on to find some vegetables.

Oliver said, "I thought of a question for Scholar Evan. I don't understand where the circle wall came from."

Franklin laughed. "Of all the complicated things you ask Father Winthrop, that's the question you want me to ask Scholar Evan?"

Oliver smiled. "No. But that was all I could think of."

Franklin laughed some more. "Nobody really knows where it came from."

"How is that possible?"

"I asked the same question when I was your age."

Oliver asked, "What did you find out?"

"Keep in mind, nothing is certain. These are just old stories passed down through the generations."

"Like The—" Oliver stopped himself before he finished saying The Word.

Franklin gave him a stern look and raised his eyebrows.

"I didn't say it." Oliver smiled. "The circle wall. Tell me what you know about that."

"They say the circle wall was here when Lady and Bruce founded Brighton."

"Why would there be a wall here?" Oliver asked. "There's no ancient city, just a few ancient buildings."

"When the Ancients were dying, it is told that some of them fled here to get away from the twisted men that were conquering the ancient cities. They built the circle wall a full mile in every direction from the center of town."

"The square?" Oliver asked.

"Of course." Franklin frowned, as though the question were stupid.

Oliver said, "That explains why there's so much ancient stone in the circle wall."

"Exactly."

"And in the places where the stones are stacked," Oliver asked, "those are the places where The People repaired it?"

"Yes. That's what I understood," said Franklin.

Oliver said, "There's another thing I don't understand. Why is it so big? Why not just build it around the town?"

"Because they needed room for fields. They had to grow crops and they had to have places for the sheep to graze. Without the wall, the demons would have destroyed everything."

"But…" Oliver thought for a moment how to ask the next question. "If the Ancients built the wall and if it really worked to keep the demons out, what happened to the Ancients that used to live in Brighton? Lady and Bruce founded Brighton with the first fifty-seven people."

"The spore," answered Franklin. "The spore took the Ancients who built the circle wall. That's why we have The Cleansing twice each year. The circle wall protects us from the demons outside, but the only way we can protect ourselves internally is to get rid of the unclean before they harm anyone."

"Couldn't we just turn them out to the forest?" Oliver asked.

Just then, a group of merchants walked by, staring at Oliver and Franklin. They spoke in hushed tones.

Franklin eyed them and then looked away. "No. We need to burn the unclean to keep safe. That is the only way."

Chapter 13: Bray

Bray peered across the campsite at the man he intended to rob. Jeremiah was snoring. Next to him, thin smoke trickled from an extinguished fire, and the skinned remains of a squirrel hung on a stick. It was well past dawn, and they were up on one of the cliffs just outside Brighton. Bray had been following the other Warden since the previous evening. Jeremiah had set up camp next to a crumbled wall of stone, probably thinking he'd be protected from demons and thieves. The man's bag was slung loosely over his shoulder, heaving up and down with each inebriated breath he took.

Jeremiah wasn't the smartest man in the wild.

Unlike Bray, Jeremiah spent his silver almost as fast as he earned it, blowing it on as much snowberry as his stomach would hold. Any money he had left over was spent at The House of Barren Women. Jeremiah wasn't even a skilled Warden. In the time Bray had known him, the man had brought in about eighty-five demon scalps—a pittance compared to the others.

And yet Brighton continued to employ him.

It was a shame, really, but the township was in no position to deny assistance. As long as demons roamed the countryside, the township would need the help of the Wardens to slay them. Each scalp netted a Warden five bits of silver—enough to fund a few decent meals.

Or in Jeremiah's case, a few more jugs of snowberry.

Goddamn louse.

Bray's anger simmered as he stared at the sleeping man. Jeremiah was a waste, really. No one would miss him if he were gone. But killing him wasn't Bray's style. He'd rather let the man live and quietly leech off his earnings.

Killing the man would be a poor investment.

Bray crept across the campsite, stepping over several loose twigs and leaves, doing his best to mask his presence. He held his knife at the ready, even though he was confident he wouldn't need it. He kept his sword in his scabbard.

In the event the man awakened, Bray had a backup plan. He'd tell Jeremiah that he'd been chasing a demon, and that he'd stumbled on the campsite. In all likelihood, Jeremiah would be too drunk and disoriented to care.

He'd probably even fall back asleep.

Bray circled the doused fire, watching the sleeping man through the thin veil of smoke. He stopped to examine the smoldering squirrel. There was still some unclaimed meat on its bones. He reached out and poked the animal. Still warm. Smiling, he plucked the leftover meat and stuffed it into his mouth, pausing for a second to chew. He'd been so busy stalking Jeremiah that he hadn't had a chance to eat.

Free food and a demon scalp. What a take.

After he scavenged the rest of the man's meal, he continued over to Jeremiah. The drunken man was still snoring, with his pack looped over one shoulder. He was clutching the strap to his chest, as if it were the pale arm of a woman instead of a dirt-stained piece of fabric. The pack was tied shut.

Damn.

That would make things more difficult.

He'd do what he had to do, and then he'd flee the area. When Jeremiah woke up, he probably wouldn't even remember he'd had a fresh scalp in his pack. Bray smirked at the thought.

He knelt down, paying close attention to the man's breathing. Up close, the snoring was even louder than he'd anticipated, which gave him ample cover to do his business. He set his knife in the dirt and reached for the strings on the pack. As he'd expected, the knot was loosely tied. After a few pulls, he tugged the pack open.

Jeremiah snorted.

He released the pack and went still. Nerves crawled through his body; his pulse raced. Jeremiah readjusted, pulling the bag over his side and out of Bray's reach. After a few seconds, he resumed snoring.

Bastard. Bray shook his head.

He'd wait another minute, just to make sure the man was asleep, and then he'd try again. His plan was to take the scalp to Davenport, where he'd hopefully trade it in for more silver than he'd get in Brighton. He already had a pack full, but another scalp would mean at least another five silver. He'd add it to his stockpile in the ruins once he got paid.

Bray shimmied closer. The pack was resting on Jeremiah's side, and it moved up and down with each alcohol-tainted breath. Bray could smell the man's body odor—a mixture of dried demon blood and unwashed sweat—and he fought the urge to vomit.

Rather than spending all his money on snowberry, the man should've bought himself a bath.

Bray reached inside the pack again, weaving his way through the fabric, grazing a few items of clothing. A shirt. Pants. He searched for anything else of value. Maybe he'd find a few bits of silver. Eventually his hand closed around the scalp. Got it. He smiled and withdrew his hand.

Before he could get it out of the pack, a large, calloused hand enveloped his wrist.

"You son of a bitch!"

Jeremiah was awake, and he wasn't happy. Bray tried to leap back, but the hand had a firm grip, and Bray lost his balance. He grabbed for his knife, but it was just out of reach.

"Jeremiah! I was just—"

"I know exactly what you were just trying to do, you goddamn thief!"

Before Bray could retort, Jeremiah punched him. The blow was sloppy, but it was powerful enough to send Bray sprawling to the ground.

Jeremiah was on his feet, advancing, eyes blazing. Bray scooted backward, crawling on hands and knees. His sword was still in his scabbard. If he could get clear of the angered man, he might be able to pull it.

Before he could make a move, Jeremiah charged him. The large man knocked into his shoulders, heaving him back to the dirt, and Bray landed hard on his tailbone. His body stung from the impact.

Jeremiah unsheathed his sword.

The last thing Bray had expected was a fight. At the same time, he'd never backed away from one, either. Before Jeremiah could descend on him, Bray lashed out with his leg, hitting the man in the ankle. Jeremiah grunted, lost his balance and tumbled.

Bray leapt to his feet.

As Jeremiah tried to recover, Bray delivered a right hook to his jaw. The man cried out in pain. Bray scooted backward. He realized he was still clutching the scalp. That was what he had come for, not a fight with a bear-sized man.

It was time to leave.

He plucked his knife from the ground and skirted toward the woods.

He dashed through the trees, listening to the intoxicated man roar behind him. Jeremiah was on his feet and was lumbering through the woods. Bray continued fleeing until Jeremiah's shouts were nothing more than complaints to an empty forest. When the man was out of earshot, Bray stopped to inspect the scalp he'd stolen.

Judging by the size and contour, the demon had been a middle-aged male. The cut was uneven, suggesting that Jeremiah had still been shaky from the fight with it. Either that or he'd already been inebriated.

Bray shrugged. A scalp is a scalp.

He opened his bag and stuffed the demon skin inside, then continued through the forest. Unlike Jeremiah, he'd been navigating the woods for most of his life, and he knew paths and shortcuts that others rarely traveled. He'd be out of harm's way before the man found him. He'd have to deal with the angered Warden later.

In front of Bray was a legion of small pines, and he weaved among them, trying to blend with the forest. He traveled softly, as usual. He varied his path slightly each time he took it, preventing a trail from forming. From the north, he could hear the faint hiss of rushing water. From the south he could hear the chatter of woodland animals. He glided in the direction of the river, intent on following it all the way to Davenport.

It was then that he heard a woman's scream.

Bray perked his ears, certain that he was hearing things. There weren't many unguided travelers in the forest, and there certainly weren't many women. Was he mistaken?

He stopped short, trying to block out the faint rush of water. After a few seconds, another scream followed. It was coming from the direction of the river. Perhaps a man was laying into his wife, or a traveler had been separated from her guide.

But something about the scream seemed different.

Although he usually didn't get involved in local disputes, the scream piqued his curiosity. He'd get close enough to see what was going on before continuing to Davenport.

Bray broke from the pines, heading toward the source of the noise.

Chapter 14: Ella

With a night's rest behind them, Ella and William took to the river with renewed strength. Although Ella's body was sore, her stomach was full, and her night in the wild had given her confidence. She'd been able to provide for William without the safety and amenities of Brighton, and that gave her hope that they'd make it a while longer. Each passing minute was a triumph in itself, and each step brought them closer to Davenport.

After walking awhile, she motioned for William to stop at the river so they could refill their flasks. He bent beside her and they untied their bags. Ella dipped her hands in the river and washed her face, letting the cool water soak her skin. Aside from the rush of the water, the forest around them was quiet.

For as long as she could remember, she'd lived among the commotion of villages and towns. Even at night, when she lay in bed, she could hear the hushed chatter of merchants or the squeak of a pushcart. This silence felt unnatural.

It took her a minute to determine the reason.

Ella smelled the creature before she saw it. If it wasn't for the breeze gusting through the trees, masking its scent with moss and mildew, she would've smelled it sooner. The sound of feet trampling brush came next. Though she was poised to flee, she feared attack was inevitable.

The monsters were fast.

She withdrew her knife.

"William, stay with me!" She grabbed the boy's arm.

William scrambled behind her, and together they crept along the riverbank, Ella clutching the blade so tightly that her hand became numb. Movement flashed through the nearby trees. A misshapen head. A wart-covered arm. It was as if the thing had decided to reveal itself in pieces, hoping to distill their fear until it could pounce.

They'd made it twenty feet further when the thing peered around a tree.

William stifled a cry when he caught sight of the monster. Ella stopped and clamped a hand over his mouth. Even though the thing was looking right at them, she had the panic-inspired thought that if they kept quiet, maybe it would move past.

Emotionless red eyes looked right at them.

The beast advanced. It tilted its head, sizing them up. Was this one of the smarter ones? Were others waiting in the trees?

Ella let go of William's mouth and tugged him along, sidestepping down the bank of the river, praying they didn't fall in the mud. To fall was to die.

She locked eyes with the beast. She could feel William shaking. She'd heard so many stories of the monsters over the years—how they moved, how they tracked, how they killed—but now that she was face-to-face with one, the stories all blurred together. Fighting it was dangerous, even if she did have a knife. She worked on gaining distance from it, stepping her way over slippery moss-covered stones to get away.

The creature stalked closer, pushing them toward the water. Each step it took revealed more of the beast's frightening appearance. Its body was covered in bloodstains and battle-wounds, its skin, filthy and bruised from years in the wild. Its joints were covered in fungal warts; its skull was swollen with the weight of infection. Its legs were long and thin; its feet, bare.

Soon she'd be forced to battle it. She'd heard what the demons could do to a man, and even worse, she'd heard what they did to women. She'd listened to stories of ravaging and disembowelment and torture—stories that were as unreal as the thing before her.

The knife suddenly felt insignificant in her hand, like a child's plaything. She wished she had a sword. She didn't know how to use one, of course, but she'd damn well try. Anything would be better than fighting the beast up close.

The thing narrowed the gap, feinting with its hands. Ella pushed William further along, trying to give him a few more steps' advantage, a few more seconds to live.

The demon was ready to lunge.

Unexpectedly, it stopped and tipped its bulbous head to the side, studying the two of them. Ella froze. The demon's eyes were unreadable, a pair of recessed orbs without feeling or compassion.

"Mom?" William whispered.

She put her finger to her lips to quiet him.

The thing stared at them, as if daring them to move. Ella swallowed and raised the knife higher, but the beast ignored it. It had no fear of weapons. The scars and gouges on its body were proof of that.

It moved its gaze to William. The boy raised his arms, as if an act of defiance might be enough to drive it back. This time Ella saw something in the beast's eyes—a glimmer of recognition, perhaps. It snarled and took a step back. It refocused on Ella.

It leapt.

Ella pushed William away. She swung the knife, slashing the creature's skin as it knocked her backward. Woman and beast pitched to the ground. Ella screamed. The creature tore at her clothes. She struggled to push it off. She felt the thing's knees digging into her, the knots of its joints jabbing her skin. It writhed and kicked, trying to subdue her. Frantic, Ella gave it a heave, and it slipped down the mossy bank and into the water. It flailed and screeched, trying to get back to shore.

"Let's go!" Ella screamed.

The boy raced down the bank. Ella jumped to her feet and ran after him. The demon splashed in the water behind them, but she dared not look back.

Something moved in the trees.

Two more beasts burst out of the underbrush. They'd been lying in wait all along. Ella and William kept running, but the demons dashed to cut them off.

Ella raised the knife, wet with the first creature's blood. Her body coursed with adrenaline, and she let out a feral cry. She pushed William behind her and slashed the air as the two approached.

"Stay back!" she shrieked, as if the things might listen.

The demons sprung. Their wart-covered arms pushed and pawed. She lost the knife as she fell to the ground. The cloying, moldering stink of their bodies threatened to suffocate her. They tore at her clothes with the same defiling hands as the guards who caught her back at the town wall. The beasts were bent on destroying her in ways she couldn't imagine.

William yelled at the beasts and stomped the ground to draw their attention.

"Run!" she screamed. "Get—"

One of the creatures inserted a bony finger in her mouth, cutting her off. She choked and gagged, then bit down. Bitter fluid spurted onto her tongue.

The beast drew back, and she got another glimpse of William, flailing at the backs of the creatures. The knife was nowhere in sight. She lifted her head and tried to get her arms free, but the demons pushed her back down. All around her were hands and limbs, and for a split second, she wondered if she'd fallen into the river and was drowning in the swift current. All she could feel was pressure and weight, and all she could do was struggle until they ripped her open.

The beasts went slack—first one, then the other.

Ella screamed as their heads toppled from their bodies. She looked up. She saw a blade, and a man with dark hair and sharp blue eyes standing behind it.

He held out his hand.

She blinked, as if she were imagining things. Had she fallen unconscious? Was she dreaming as she was dying?

"Are you okay?" the man asked.

She nodded, though she wasn't sure. Ignoring the offered hand, she struggled to right herself. Her body felt stiff and weak, but the adrenaline of battle still coursed through her.

As she rose, she got a better look at him. His clothes were ragged, his face was dirt-stained, and it looked like he hadn't had a bath in weeks. His cheeks were flecked with stubble.

William was standing behind him.

"What are you two doing out here?" the man asked.

"We were just—" she fumbled for the right words.

"Did you lose your guide?"

She nodded, too rattled to think of a story.

William flew to her side, putting a hand to her belly. "Mom."

Ella saw the distress on his face. She wasn't hurt. At least she didn't think so. She looked down. She was covered in so much blood that she couldn't help but check for wounds.

There were none.

The blood belonged to the demons whose heads lay sightless and still on the ground at her feet.

"I'm okay," she said as she crept away from the monsters' decapitated bodies. Remembering the third beast, the one that attacked her first, Ella looked back down the bank.

"They're dead," the man assured her. "All three of them."

He sheathed his sword, knelt down, and grabbed hold of one of the heads. He pulled out his knife and began separating the scalp.

"I've heard stories about them..." Ella said. "That they come back..."

The man stopped and looked up at her, furrowing his brow. "Back from the dead?" He laughed loudly and went back to his gory business. "Not everything you hear is true. A girl your age should know that."

She opened her mouth to argue, but the man had stolen her thoughts and put them into words, as if she were little more than a child caught in the ruins. She kept silent, watching him separate skin from bone, cleaning his knife on the grass between cuts.

"I'm Bray," he said, without looking up.

William let go of his mother. "Are you a Warden?" he asked.

"Yes." He went to work on the second head.

"I want to be a Warden. But Mom says—"

Ella shushed him and pulled him back to her. The kneeling man stopped what he was doing and grinned.

"What does she say?"

William looked at his mother, then back at the hunter. "She says being a Skin-Seller isn't a noble profession."

Bray laughed. He wiped his face and returned to the scalp. When he finished cutting it free, he scraped off the excess skin with his blade. Ella watched with a mixture of curiosity and revulsion. In death, the creatures were just as grotesque as before, but less menacing, at least. She glanced over at the bodies. The severed necks still pumped fluid onto the riverbank, and the stench permeated the air, as if the soil had ingested the creatures' blood.

That same blood was all over her hands and clothing. A jab of fear coursed through her as she looked down at herself.

"Don't worry, you won't get infected," Bray said, as if reading her mind. "Lucky for you, it's not flowering season. A couple of weeks from now—" Bray looked at the bodies. "I wouldn't have bothered with you."

He opened his pack, stuffed the scalps inside, and then resealed it. He slung it over his back. "Where are you two headed?"

"Davenport," Ella answered.

"Is your guide still alive?"

"I-I think so."

"If you'd like, I'll help you find him. I know the area. He can't be far."

"We'll be fine," Ella said.

"Where did you lose him?"

"That way." She pointed vaguely up the riverbank. "We should have no problem finding him. We'll just get moving and I'm sure he'll catch up."

William was still watching the Warden intently. She tugged his arm, snapping him from his trance, pulling him along. The last thing she needed was further interrogation. They'd take their chances on their own. She waited until she'd gone about twenty paces before she glanced over her shoulder.

"Thank you, Bray," she called back to the man.

As nice as he seemed, she was hesitant to trust anybody right now. She'd heard stories about Wardens—stories almost as frightening as the stories about the beasts. Even in town, she did her best to stay away from them. Bray was sliding his knife back into his sheath. She eyed him warily, but he made no moves to come after them.

She turned back around and continued walking, keeping her eyes on the trees. The forest seemed darker than before, as if conspiring to hide beasts within.

She'd only gone a few more steps when Bray called after them.

"You might want to get your story straight in case you run into someone else out here." He paused and added: "Guides don't come out of the towns this close to flowering season."

Ella kept walking without responding. She shuffled William along, her heart pattering at a frantic rhythm. She should've thought her story through as she and William were hiking through the forest. She needed something more plausible.

What if the man turned them in?

She picked up her pace. Footsteps squished through the soft ground behind them. She swallowed. Was the man following them?

The footsteps grew louder. The man was jogging to catch up. Why wouldn't he leave them alone? All she wanted was to get to Davenport and—

"You forgot something!"

When she looked back, Bray was standing there, her blade in his hand. He passed it to her. She'd left it at the riverbank. Dammit. *What a fool I am.*

"Thanks," she said.

His face was calm and even, and she read no ill intent.

"Listen, I'm heading to Davenport myself. It'd be silly for us to travel separately," he said. "Especially with the two of you by yourselves."

She struggled to think of an argument, but couldn't.

Bray continued. "You'll never last a night out here," he added. "I know the wild better than anyone you're likely to meet. I promise I won't hurt you or the boy."

She studied his face, as if she'd somehow be able to peer into his thoughts and determine his motives. What if he behaved like the guards back at the wall? What if he was lying? At the same time, she knew he was right. They couldn't go it alone. Their encounter with the demons was proof. She rolled the knife in her hands.

Both William and Bray were watching her, waiting for a response.

"Okay," she said finally.

A thin smile flitted across William's face. She patted the boy's head and joined the Warden.

Chapter 15: Oliver

Oliver placed the pot of rabbit stew next to the loaf of bread in the center of the table for the midday meal. He took the empty chair next to Father Nelson. Trying not to be rude and stare hungrily at the food—it seemed to be one of Father Winthrop's favorite peeves—he focused his attention across the table at Franklin, who seemed to be excessively concerned about maintaining at least a small gap between himself and Winthrop's great belly, which had a tendency to spread out and crowd whomever had the misfortune to sit next to him.

Each of the four placed their hands on the table astride their empty bowls. Father Winthrop looked at each place setting, took a deep breath, and in a pompous tone Oliver had heard too often, started his chant. "Let no man hunger while other men eat. A man alone cannot survive unless all men survive. For no man can stand against the demon beasts alone. In the tradition of the first fifty-seven, we share this meal with whomever is within these walls."

"Well said," each of the other three mumbled, as tradition required.

Father Winthrop ladled two helpings in his bowl, and then gave the same to Father Nelson. He reached for the bread while Franklin scooted his and Oliver's much smaller bowls over beside the stew pot. Father Winthrop gave them each a single serving.

When the soup was poured, Winthrop tore a shred of crust off the loaf and set it next to Franklin.

"Thank you, Father," Franklin said softly, lowering his eyes.

Winthrop tore a great chunk out of the loaf's center and passed the remainder to Father Nelson.

Nelson nodded and tore off a similar crusted end for Oliver. "It is good to see the traditions respected here," Nelson said.

Father Winthrop nodded smugly, but then his facial expression changed, as though he might be offended. He asked, "How do you mean, Father Nelson?"

Nelson leaned over his bowl, and in a conspiratorial voice said, "Many in Coventry no longer share their meals. They hoard their food for themselves and their families. I fear this tradition is dying."

Father Winthrop slurped a big spoonful of the lumpy brown soup. "Tradition and faith are the stones and mortar upon which our society is built. Without those—" Winthrop shrugged, letting his sentence hang in the air to finish itself. He bit a chunk of bread.

Nelson nodded pensively. Franklin copied the gesture. Oliver took a bite of his dry piece of bread crust.

Winthrop waggled his spoon across the table at Nelson and added, "When tradition falls by the wayside, it is the fault of the clergy, is it not, Father Nelson?"

Nelson froze mid bite, clearly not having expected his gossipy bit of news to be turned back on him. "I—"

Winthrop shook his head and looked down at his stew, took a bite, looked back up and caught each eye at the table before focusing on Nelson. "The Word is the source of all the powerful truths by which we live, Father Nelson. I should not have to tell you this."

"No, Father Winthrop," Nelson replied.

"Respect for tradition must be taught with The Word. In Brighton, we all know the responsibility for teaching The

Word to the peasants falls to one man." Winthrop drilled Nelson with his eyes.

"Yes, Father Winthrop. I understand that the failings of my flock are my failings as a guide and teacher of The Word."

"Indeed," Winthrop agreed. "Sometimes grave actions must be taken, like the spiking General Blackthorn intends for this afternoon."

After that, everyone ate silently for a bit, until Oliver looked innocently across the table at Father Winthrop and asked, "Was it the original fifty-seven survivors that started the tradition of equally sharing their food?"

Winthrop scooped another load of broth into his mouth.

Oliver looked down at his tiny bowl, letting his gaze linger before looking back up for an answer.

Franklin kicked Oliver under the table.

Winthrop harrumphed and put down his spoon. "Of course, Oliver, my boy. We don't chant our dinner prayer to whet our appetites; we do it to remind ourselves of our traditions. In this case we must remember that in the old days food was scarce. The first fifty-seven—"

"Or," Father Nelson interrupted, "you might say, the last fifty-seven?"

"The last?" Franklin asked.

"Yes," Father Nelson answered, "the last of the Ancients to survive. The fifty-seven were the last survivors of the ancient race of men and the forefathers of all of us in the three townships."

"I've never thought of it that way," Franklin said.

"Yes, the last, the first, the same," Winthrop confirmed for everyone. "The fifty-seven—the only men left on the great flat earth—knew that if men were once again to have dominion over all, they needed to endeavor together.

Judging by the count of men in the three townships, I dare say the tradition has served us well."

"Well said," Father Nelson nodded.

"Well said," Franklin and Oliver parroted.

After eating several bites of his flavorless stew—cooked that way to meet Father Winthrop's tastes— Oliver asked Father Nelson, "Was there really a Lady and Bruce? Were they real people?"

Father Nelson swallowed, looked at Father Winthrop who shook his head slightly and rolled his eyes. Father Nelson said, "The story of Lady and Bruce is my favorite of all the tales. Yes, they were real."

Oliver laid his spoon beside his half-full bowl. He shuffled around in his seat to more comfortably face Father Nelson.

Franklin scowled and kicked Oliver again.

Oliver bit his tongue on the verbal skewering he was plotting for Father Nelson and thought about the orphanage.

And no matter how many times everyone said the orphanage was a good place for children whose parents had been Cleansed or died naturally, Oliver knew it wasn't. He'd visited that squalid building with Franklin and Father Winthrop, had seen the sunken cheeks, smelled the stink of the unwashed, felt the hopelessness of the empty-eyed children there. No, the orphanage was a rancid, evil place where the traditions about sharing never ventured.

Father Nelson put a hand on Oliver's shoulder. It was that comforting hand that the Fathers put on the ignorant, a gesture that said, "Listen to me, my simple brother, and I'll shed the light of faith on you."

Like most people in Brighton, Oliver didn't like it when others touched him. It made him imagine little red demon spores crawling over his skin. But the condescension in that touch was just as disgusting.

Father Nelson asked, "Why do you question the stories of Lady and Bruce?"

In a childish, sing-song voice, the kind that always worked to lure Father Winthrop into a trap of his own contradictions, Oliver asked, "I don't doubt the stories are true. I simply envy your certainty. That's all. I don't know if I can ever possess such faith."

Father Nelson chuckled.

Father Winthrop sat his bowl on the table after drinking the last of the broth and pointed at Father Nelson. "This one knows the truth, young Oliver."

"Knows? Not believes but knows?" Oliver asked.

"Yes, my boy." Father Nelson leaned back in his chair, steepled his fingers and looked smugly down his nose at each of those around the table. "You know the story of the emergence, do you not?"

"Of course, every child knows that story." Oliver had a gift for conveying confidence and innocence in the same breath.

"Tell me what you know."

Oliver looked down at his bowl. He fidgeted for a second with his bread. Oliver said, "My mother told me the story when I was a child and afraid of monsters in the dark. But my mother was just a peasant. Her version of the story was a peasant's incomplete version." Oliver looked across the table. "Father Winthrop has not had time in my teachings to bless me with that story. Perhaps now would be a good time."

"Yes," Father Nelson agreed immediately.

Franklin jumped in on the consensus. "I would like that as well."

Feigning modesty, Father Winthrop said, "Well, if you insist."

They did, and Father Winthrop began his tale.

Chapter 16: Ella

Ella, Bray, and William followed the riverbank. On Bray's suggestion, they kept to the woods, using the water as a guide. According to the Warden, the demons often drank from its waters. The thick trunks of trees provided a natural barrier, but every so often Ella glimpsed the water through the foliage, and the rush of the current was never far from her ears.

She surveyed the tops of the trees, expecting to see movement in the branches. She'd heard stories about the creatures of the wild—not just demons, but other predators, as well.

The travelers remained quiet as they walked. For a long while the only sounds keeping them company were the swaying wind rifling through the tree branches, the occasional splash of a river turtle, and the snaps of twigs underfoot.

They were startled by a crack in the underbrush. Bray held up his hand, warning them to be still. Something brown was lingering in a patch of scrub brush about fifty yards away. A nervous tremor shot through Ella's body, and her hand blanched on the knife. Was it another demon? It didn't look like one. She could only see pieces of the animal through the green leaves ahead—an elongated neck and nose, patches of smooth brown fur. The animal had gone as still as them. She stared until she could make out a single round eye. The animal was standing sideways.

Both the travelers and the animal remained quiet, as if neither were willing to admit the other's presence. After a tense moment, the animal lifted its head and sniffed the air. Then it bounded off in the opposite direction.

Ella listened to the crinkle of underbrush as it made its departure. "What was that?" she whispered to Bray.

"A deer."

She stared after it in wonder. "A deer? I thought they were extinct."

Bray shook his head. "There are some, but not many. The demons killed nearly all of them. To see one is rare, indeed."

"Have you ever hunted one?" William asked.

"No. The meat and hide would fetch a hefty price at the butcher's, but I've never killed one. Wardens believe killing one is bad luck."

The boy nodded. William's brow was pursed with curiosity, and for a moment, Ella was able to forget he was infected and pretend he was as normal as any other boy.

She peered through the wild to catch another glimpse of the deer, but there was no longer any sign of it. Ella tried to recreate the image in her head. Her hope was to hold onto it, so that she might recount the tale later.

With the encounter over, Bray led them through a thick section of pines, one hand on his knife, the other on his sheathed sword. With each step, Ella grew more grateful that she'd chosen to follow him. Although she still didn't trust him fully, the Warden's protection was worth the risk, at least for now.

The swell of the river had died down, and while they walked, Bray began to narrate some of his encounters with the beasts. The enraptured William hung on every word.

"So it isn't true the demons can come back to life?" William asked.

"That's just a tale," answered Bray.

"So all of them can be killed?"

"Yes. The same as you or me."

Bray pointed to the pack on his shoulders. "Do you know how many scalps this pack has seen?"

The boy shook his head.

"One thousand, two hundred and eighty-one."

Wide-eyed, William asked, "You counted all of them?"

"Yep. Every one."

"What about the ones you took today?"

"Of course. They're included."

William looked amazed. "What happens when the demons go extinct? What will you do then?"

Bray paused, as if he'd never been asked the question before. "Their numbers are thin, that's for sure. But I've heard rumors of many more coming in from the south."

"Do you believe the rumors?" William asked.

Bray patted his stomach. "I have to, if I want to eat."

He grinned and continued through the trees.

Ella watched the man. She'd seen several of Bray's kind come to Brighton, visiting the brothel, loitering on the sidewalks and streets, spending silver on whatever distractions they could find. But she'd rarely talked to them.

The only run-ins she'd had with them were the occasional men who purchased her wares directly. Normally she sold her roots and berries to the merchants. In those few instances when she'd spoken with a Warden, her conversations had been brief, focused on the transaction at hand. She seldom looked at the men's faces, and rarely made eye contact.

She wondered if Bray had been one of them. Did he recognize her? Would it make a difference if he did? He already knew they were on the run.

If he were going to turn them in, he'd have done it by now.

She hoped to God he didn't discover William's secret. She'd do anything to prevent that from happening. If Bray found out, there was no telling what he'd do. What would William be worth to him? Another five bits of silver?

Stop it, Ella.

The thought was so vile that she swallowed it back. Bray was several steps ahead of them, scouting the path before they walked it.

He doesn't know anything, and he won't find out, she tried to convince herself.

She reached for William's hand and pulled him close, just in case.

Chapter 17: Oliver

Oliver waited for Father Winthrop to begin his story. Father Winthrop sat back in his chair and scooted away from the table. He apparently needed room for gestures and such.

All eyes rested on him, waiting patiently for him to speak. Father Winthrop bathed his ego in the silent attention before he finally began. "The world of old was a magical, terrible place. Men constructed buildings of stone and steel that touched the clouds."

"Steel?" Oliver asked. He'd never heard that part. "Were they rich?"

"Men had so much steel in those days that they could make things you can't even imagine."

Father Nelson put the hand back on Oliver's shoulder. "Let Father Winthrop tell his story."

"No, no," Father Winthrop said, "It's okay. The questions do not bother me. They are part of the boys' education." And, Oliver knew, they left Father Winthrop at the center of attention longer. "Men had devices that flew them through the air like birds. They had wheeled carriages that propelled them from city to city at speeds faster than any horse could dream of running, faster than any bird could hope to fly."

Stories of the time before God gave the world to the demons always left Oliver dubiously awed.

"Men had weapons that blazed fire and steel and could kill a thousand demons in a moment. Men owned the lightning and the thunder."

"But it escaped," Oliver blurted, unable to contain his excitement. "That's what my mother said, before she went to the pyre."

"Yes, it did escape," Winthrop confirmed. "It lives in the clouds now, tormenting farmers, sometimes blowing down houses, sometimes burning barns." Father Winthrop took a long drink from his cup. "The Ancients had the power to kill by the thousands, nay, the millions. But God was unhappy with man for creating such wickedness."

"Millions?" Oliver asked. There was much to the story that his mother and father hadn't known. "Why would they need to be so powerful?"

"In those days, the number of men on the great flat world was beyond imagination. The people of different cities fought and killed one another and grew so powerful that they believed they were equal to God. The Ancients believed that they were gods themselves. They told themselves that they no longer needed The Word, and as forgiving and loving as God was, he could not forgive that sin. So God opened Hell and spilled the demons free."

"All of the twisted men came from Hell?" Oliver asked.

"Most of them, yes." Father Winthrop nodded. "Many men were turned to demons, themselves. The demons killed nearly all the rest. The only way for men to survive in those days was to escape the demons, and the only place left to go where there were no demons was Hell. You see, they'd all left to come live on the earth."

"I don't understand that part," Oliver said, having lost any thoughts about teasing Winthrop into a fluster.

"If I may, Father Winthrop." Father Nelson sat up in his seat and leaned on the table.

Father Winthrop frowned, showing his reluctance to give up the spotlight. Nevertheless, he granted the floor to Father Nelson.

Nelson looked at each of the boys, "They say some stories contain metaphors to simplify the concepts, to make things easier to understand in these less magical times."

Oliver's brow crinkled. "I don't understand. Are you saying the Ancients didn't hide in Hell?"

"Hell can be many things," Father Nelson said.

"Yes," Father Winthrop confirmed, as if the words needed his blessing to be true. "In those dark times when the demons overran the great cities, there were one man and one woman in all of the great flat world who were not arrogant, were not drunk on the power of their magic."

"Lady and Bruce," Oliver blurted.

"Of course," Father Winthrop nodded. "Lady and Bruce, among all people, were not enamored with the magic of their world, though they did know how to use it. They descended to Hell. Some say it was the real Hell. Others, as Father Nelson have suggested, believe that Hell is a metaphor. He can tell you more about that when I finish. Either way, Lady and Bruce stayed in Hell for seven years."

"Seven years?" Oliver asked. His mother had said seven seasons. His grandfather had told him seven days. All those numbers seemed ridiculous to Oliver. How could anyone live underground in Hell for so long? "Was the old magic that powerful?"

"Yes," Father Winthrop said, "Perhaps another metaphor, perhaps not. When Lady and Bruce left Hell, choosing once again to walk in the world of demons, they believed they were alone and they despaired. They believed they would be the last two humans ever to live."

"I never understood that part." Oliver interrupted, "Why didn't they just have children?"

"Lady was barren," said Winthrop.

That made Oliver a little sad. Barren women were of little use, except as prostitutes.

"Though Lady was barren," said Winthrop, "she was strong. Together with Bruce, they built a safe place back in the world where they could defend themselves and grow crops. That place was called Brighton. Over time, other people found Lady and Bruce and settled here to live with them, seventy-seven in all."

"But I always thought it was fifty-seven?" Oliver said, on the hunt for a contradiction.

Fathers Nelson and Winthrop smiled.

Oliver looked back and forth between them, sensing their arrogance.

Father Winthrop broke the silence. "There were many in the original seventy-seven who were jealous of Lady. It is said that it was their fault that Lady's name was lost to history. Lady was an unusual woman. She was stronger than any man. Men with soft, weak hearts hated her for that."

"I never knew any of this," Oliver muttered.

Father Winthrop shared a knowing look with Father Nelson and said, "If only she could have had children, what a strong race of men we would be now."

"What happened to the soft-hearted men?" Oliver asked.

"Arguments, hatred, and fights. The soft-hearted men hated Lady and Bruce."

"Fights?" Oliver asked. "The soft-hearted men fought with a woman? Fist fights?"

"Yes." Winthrop glanced at Nelson before answering, paused, and said, "No man could beat Lady in a fist fight."

Oliver gulped. "Wow. I don't know what to say about that."

"It is difficult for most men to accept," said Winthrop. "That is why we don't tell those parts of the story in our devotional service. Most men cannot accept it."

Oliver understood. "So the soft-hearted men got tired of being shamed by a woman and they left?"

"Lady and Bruce exiled them. After that, there were fifty-seven, the first of the clean ones. We are all descended from them." Father Winthrop picked up a hunk of bread and bit off a large piece, as if needing to replenish his energy.

Father Nelson took over the conversation, as if he and Father Winthrop had practiced the handoff several times before. "Many years ago, when I was not much older than Franklin here, I went with Father Winthrop's predecessor and a half dozen other faithful men on a pilgrimage to find Hell."

Oliver shuddered. Franklin grimaced.

"You see," said Nelson, "Father Winthrop's predecessor believed in the metaphorical Hell. He believed that the place where Lady and Bruce spent their seven years below the earth was a real place, and he believed that it was a place not far from here. That makes sense, right? If they were going to build the first town after the fall of the Ancients, why travel far from their refuge to do so?"

Shaking his head, unable to hide his disbelief, Oliver asked, "Even if this place was real, how could Father Bristol hope to find it? The earth is, well…big, I guess, and demons are everywhere."

Father Nelson put his condescending hand back on Oliver's shoulder. "Father Bristol said he possessed a secret knowledge. He never told me or anyone else what that was, or where he got it. He said he'd tell me after the pilgrimage."

"But he didn't?" Oliver asked.

"You're jumping ahead," said Nelson.

"Sorry."

"We journeyed into the mountains in the east. Of the six of us, two died from demon bite on the way."

Oliver interrupted, "They turned to demons?"

Nelson shook his head. "They were murdered and eaten." Nelson looked distantly at the bowl in front of him, but shook off the memory and picked the story back up. "We searched the mountain all through the summer and into the winter. We were up on the mountain in the deep snow, thinking we'd perish, when we stumbled upon something strange."

"What was it? What did you stumble upon?" asked Oliver.

Nelson leaned over the table and let the suspense build as he looked around at them. "A steel door."

"A door made of steel?" Franklin's tone made it clear that he didn't believe it.

Nelson nodded cockily.

"A whole door, the whole thing made of steel?" asked Oliver.

"Yes," said Nelson.

"Was it a small door?" Oliver shook his head. Surely a door made of such precious metal couldn't be large.

Nelson leaned back and spread his hands. "No, a large door, as wide as a man can reach with outstretched arms."

"No," Oliver whispered.

"I saw it myself. Touched it myself." Nelson looked at Franklin and then back at Oliver.

Oliver said, "With that much steel, you could be rich."

"Yes, I could. But it was not riches that we sought; at least, not riches of this earth. We sought spiritual riches on our pilgrimage."

"Did you open the door?" Oliver asked.

Father Winthrop said, "Let the man finish his story, boy."

"Yes, Father."

"We didn't need to open the door," said Nelson." It was made of heavy, thick steel, but time had rusted it through in places, and we were each able to squeeze inside through the holes."

"What did you find?"

"At first we thought it was a cave."

"A cave with a door?" Oliver grinned.

Nelson shrugged and continued. "We realized that the walls were made by man, both of old, rusted steel, and Ancient Stone. There were artifacts, made by the hand of man, some for no purpose that we could discern, others that we could. We found jars and bottles with strange markings."

Oliver was rapt.

"But the strangest, most wonderful thing of all, was a room that we discovered through a door in the corner of this strange place."

"And what was in it?" Oliver asked.

"The door into that room was in better condition than the one that led into the shelter, being out of the weather, I suspect. When we let ourselves inside, we saw ancient and rotted artifacts on the floor, as we saw in the other room, but the most amazing thing was that the walls were painted in faded, flaking paint." Father Nelson paused. "And everyone knows that in the legend of Lady and Bruce, Lady was a painter."

Father Nelson looked around at his small audience, ensuring that he had everyone's full attention. "The murals on the wall showed two people wearing strange clothing. The garments looked to have been made of leaves, and were of multiple colors of the forest. In some places the coloring on the clothes looked so similar to the background trees and bushes, it was hard to see if the figures were people or not. Their arms and faces were the only parts not covered with the cloth. In one mural, they were fighting the monsters and killing many. There were parts of the painting that showed the two living in the magical city, and showed them hunting the animals of the forest."

"How did you know it was Lady and Bruce?" Oliver asked.

"At first, we didn't. The pictures of the two people appeared to match the descriptions of the two from the legend. But in each picture, they both appeared to be men. At least that's what we all thought. That is, until we came across a section of one of the murals where they were both naked and holding hands in a field of beautiful flowers. Well, I guess the flowers were beautiful before they were faded by time. But that confirmed it for us. The two naked people were definitely a man and a woman, Lady and Bruce."

Chapter 18: Ella

After conversation with the Warden had died down, Ella focused on her surroundings. Other than the faint rush of the river's current, she could hear the chirps and chatter of birds, and the sound was soothing. Despite her circumstances, she felt freer than she had in a while—perhaps freer than she'd ever been.

Gone were the confines of the guard, the commanding presence of the Elders, and the threat of Blackthorn's men. All rules had been stripped away, leaving her alone with her decisions.

How nice it would be to build a house in the wild, to make one's own way.

If it weren't for the monsters lurking in the woods, the feeling of freedom might've overwhelmed her with joy. But another thought kept lingering in her mind.

Soon William would be one of them.

She squeezed her son's hand tighter, savoring the minutes. She'd protect him to the end. Whatever that took, however long he had, she'd be there for him.

The guards would be after them soon. Ella and William needed to hurry. If they were caught, all the freedom they'd gained would be stripped away.

They followed the Warden for half of a day, until the sun transformed from yellow to orange and the tree branches started to blend with the forest. Bray broke the silence.

"We'll need to take shelter soon. Are you hungry?" he asked.

"A little," Ella admitted.

"Do you have food?"

She thought of the berries in her bag. Although she had enough food for three people, she was hesitant to share. Who knew how long it would need to last?

"Not much."

"Don't worry about me—I've already eaten."

At the prospect of stopping, Ella instinctively glanced behind them, half-expecting a troop of men on their heels, or a pack of demons, but the forest was empty.

"Don't worry. We'll be concealed," Bray said. "Nightfall is coming, and we won't want to stay out past sunset. Follow me. I know a place where we can stay."

Bray took a turn through the trees. He wound through brush and bramble and up an incline, navigating a bed of loose stone.

"Be quiet," Bray warned, as William tumbled a few rocks noisily underfoot.

Ella and William followed his lead, stepping lightly, gaining elevation with each step. Before long, they were on top of a grass-covered hill. Several ancient stones marked the perimeter, lined up in a rectangular formation. In the center of the stones was a recessed hole, about ten feet deep. The bottom was covered in tall weeds and ivy.

"Was there a building here?" she asked.

Bray nodded. "Yes. A long time ago."

Bray walked the perimeter, peering off the small hill and into the surrounding forest. After a few minutes surveillance, he proclaimed that they were safe. He pointed to a half-crumbled wall and directed them to crouch behind it.

"Rest here and eat. Then we'll hole up before dark."

He scratched his chin, and then stationed himself nearby. Ella and William followed his instruction and dipped behind the wall. She unslung her pack and dug into it, keeping a close eye on the Warden, but he wasn't showing any interest in them. He was busy glancing over the hill.

"I'm not hungry," William told Ella, almost immediately.

"You have to eat," she stated.

She opened the flaps and began digging for a pouch of dried berries. She found one in the bottom of the pack. Among the food pouches was another containing her silver. She buried it underneath some clothes, then scooped out a handful of fruit and reached out to William. He kept his hands at his sides.

"William!" she snapped, giving him a stern look. It was the look she reserved for the rare occasions when he wouldn't tidy the house, or when she had trouble rousing him in the morning.

"It doesn't matter anymore, Mom."

"Of course it matters. You need to eat."

"But pretty soon I'll be—"

Her eyes widened and she made a grab for him, and William silenced himself immediately. She snuck a peek at Bray. He was still standing ten feet away, looking out over the trees and hills. It didn't appear he'd heard anything. Still, there was no way to be sure.

"We'll talk later," she said quietly.

She retrieved a handful of berries and popped them in her mouth, chewing out of habit rather than hunger. After a few moments of silence, Bray wandered from his post and back over to them.

"How're you feeling?" he asked.

"Fine," Ella said, keeping her eyes on her bag.

"I was just checking. A lot of townsfolk aren't used to the exercise."

She snuck a look at him, and saw that he was smirking.

"We get plenty of it," she retorted.

Ella felt a tinge of annoyance. Between her time spent gathering and her daily rounds to the merchants, she was in better shape than most. Maybe even better than when she'd tended the farm with Ethan. Rather than explaining herself, she kept quiet.

Right now, it was better to be annoyed than afraid.

When William finished his food, he stood, dusting the dirt from his pants, and surveyed the horizon. Ella noticed he'd lost his look of resignation. She packed the remaining berries back in her bag and stood.

Bray was pointing at a mountain in the distance.

"Do you see that?" he asked.

Ella and William nodded.

"That's what we call Wanderer's Peak."

"Is that where we're going?" William asked.

"Not now. We'd never make it before nightfall. Tomorrow evening we'll stay there."

"Why is it called Wanderer's Peak?"

"It's the highest point between Brighton and Davenport. A lot of the Wardens use it for safety. It gives us a better view of the demons. Better than here."

"Will other Wardens be there?" Ella asked, trying to mask her concern.

Bray shrugged. "We'll see. I have a spot of my own up there that nobody knows about. So either way, we don't have to worry about finding a place to sleep tomorrow." He looked up at the sun, which was starting to descend.

"Where are we staying tonight?"

"Right here," he said.

Bray pointed down into the square hole beside where they'd eaten.

Ella followed the line of his finger down. "What am I looking at?"

"You can barely see it," he said, "But down there, behind that debris is an ancient door that leads to a room."

Ella asked, "Do you mean a room built by the Ancients?"

Bray looked at Ella like she had just asked him the stupidest of questions. "Of course."

"The demons." Ella looked around nervously. "They live in ruins like these."

Bray laughed heartily. "Is that what you've heard? That they have their own houses?"

Ella glared at him. This Warden was going to be hard to like.

"Not all ruins," said Bray. "Just in the ancient city."

"Are you sure?" she asked.

"I'm sure." Bray turned and pointed at Wanderer's peak. "If we try to make it to the peak we won't get there until well after midnight. Travelling through the forest at night is not wise. If we spend the night here, we'll be safe."

Ella stared into the debris. "Or you'll murder us and leave our bodies inside the room."

Bray laughed loudly again. "Why would I need to murder you down there and foul a perfectly good hideout with your corpses? Wouldn't I have been better off to let the monsters kill you by the river?"

Ella looked down into the hole and gasped. While her and Bray were talking, William had climbed down and cracked the door. He was peeking behind the debris into a dark hole in the side of the rectangle. "William. Get back here. Now!"

William looked back up, smiled, and slipped out of sight.

"No." Ella looked left and right at the walls of the big square hole, looking for an obvious way down.

Bray jumped into the hole, rolled to the ground and bounced back up to his feet. He pointed at the thick wall of vines. "Climb down there."

Looking at the depth of the hole, Ella knew she'd break an ankle if she jumped. She ran around to the other side of the hole and scrambled down the wall, scratching herself and tearing her dress on the way.

Once her feet hit solid ground, she turned to see Bray squeezing through the opened door, which was hidden behind some kind of fallen support beam. It seemed to be going into the earth. "Bray?"

He didn't turn around.

She bounded across the small space and squeezed behind the support beam and through the door. "William? William?"

Inside the dark room, she smelled smoke and ashes. Once her eyes adjusted, she saw Bray's silhouette.

"William's here," Bray said. "He's fine."

She shuffled forward though she could barely make out the floor. When she reached William, she grasped his shoulder and turned him around. "What were you thinking?"

He looked up at her with a question on his shadowed face. "What?"

"What are you doing running off without me?"

He shook his head. "I was exploring."

Calming her frantic breathing she said, "Don't do that. You can't explore when you're outside the circle wall. Demons could've been in here. You could've—"

"What?" William asked. "There are no demons in here."

Bray was looking around in the semi-darkness. "He's right. They don't come down here."

"You can't know that," Ella told William.

"I know," William replied.

Ella shook her head and drew an exasperated breath as she took in the darkened room. Through the faint light from the doorway, she could make out the cracks in the walls. The room was larger then her house back in Brighton and full of debris. "How could you know demons weren't down here?"

William pointed out through the door they'd come through. "Nothing on the ground outside was disturbed. No tracks, no broken twigs. Even the autumn leaves weren't crunched like they'd been stepped on."

"He's right about that," said Bray.

Ella laughed and ran her hand through William's hair. "A day and a half in the wild and now you're a tracker."

William's face turned serious as he shook his head. "I notice things, Mom. I'm a kid, but I notice things."

"You don't even know what demon footprints look like." Ella bent over to bring her face level with William's. "How would you know the difference between a demon foot print and a person's footprint? How could you know that the demons hadn't been careful when they snuck in so they could ambush the next person who came through the door?"

William pushed his mom's hand off his head. "I saw their tracks in the forest yesterday and today. You didn't notice them, but I did."

Ella looked worriedly up at Bray, as though he might say something to prove William's words untrue. She said, "William, how come you didn't say anything to me?"

"You were already frightened," he answered. "I didn't want to scare you anymore. I wanted to protect you."

Ella engulfed the boy in a hug and sniffled. "It's my job to protect you, honey."

Bray moved away from them. "I'll start a fire. It may get cold tonight." He shuffled through the scraps of wood and other things on the floor, collecting what looked like it might burn.

Ella let go of William.

William said, "I learned about the tracks as we were walking through the forest."

"Just by walking through the forest?" Ella wasn't sure whether to believe William or not.

He shrugged. "There wasn't anything else to do so I paid attention. I learned that the twisted men don't wear shoes. Not like us."

"That's true," Bray added.

"Okay," Ella conceded. She recalled the demons they'd encountered at the river. They'd all been barefoot.

"And," William said, "They don't try to hide. They move like predators through the forest. They don't need to disguise their tracks."

"True again," Bray said. "They don't fear anything in the forest."

Shaking her head, Ella asked William, "And you learned this all by yourself? Just from looking at their tracks?"

"Yes, Mom," William answered. "It's easy. All you have to do is pay attention."

"Why don't we get some sleep," Bray interrupted them. "The demons are more active at night. Whether they come down here or not, we don't want to alert them."

Ella nodded. She stared back into the darkness for William, but he had already crouched down and begun opening his pack.

Chapter 19: Minister Beck

The soft pale stones of Brighton's plaza seemed to drink in the stench of ash and burned flesh. For weeks after a Cleansing, the air leached the smells back out of the rocks and tormented passersby with the memories of that day. For that reason, Beck made a habit of avoiding the square for a fortnight after a Cleansing. He didn't even enter the square on market days, when the farmers brought their produce in from the fields to sell.

Unfortunately, circumstances required Beck to now pass through the plaza just two days after The Cleansing. In the middle of the day with the sun heating its flat stones, it reeked of death, both burned and rotting. The smell brought to mind too many acrid, clingy memories — images and sounds Beck tried hard to forget.

So much unnecessary suffering.

Such dogmatic adherence to stories passed by word of mouth, stories passed from one generation of illiterate holy men to the next generation of novices. And so it went.

Beck never understood the faith that Father Winthrop's imbecilic lot put in a collection of unwritten stories. Perhaps they'd been true when they'd first been whispered into a zealot's ear so many generations ago, but they'd likely morphed, whether through faded memory, translation, or malicious choice.

Any child burned by gossip the first time knew that to be true.

When Beck had raised the point to Winthrop, the Bishop had indignantly explained that the Holy Words of God were meant to be fluid. Winthrop said that God revealed to men only as much of his plan as men needed to hear, and that changes in the Words from one generation to the next were part of God's mechanism for parsing out the light of his wisdom in portions that men were able to consume. How dare Beck imply that anything else might be occurring?

The best part of it all was that Father Winthrop seemed to have been inventing the explanation on the fly, as if his mere assertion of the theory made it part of the holy verbal canon.

How ironically imperfect religion was. The holy men were never wrong.

Beck rolled his eyes and glanced to his right. Scholar Evan, his apprentice, had fallen behind. Evan was paying too much attention to the long the row of spikes that lined the plaza. Each spike was a sharpened pole that stood several feet taller than a man. The spikes were topped with the heads of Ella Barrow's friends and acquaintances.

And Blackthorn wasn't finished yet.

According to the census, the last of Ella's relations, her aunt and uncle, lived in Davenport, a small frontier village on the banks of a wide river.

"Are you well, Evan?" Beck asked.

"Yes, Minister. I am troubled. My troubles slow my feet."

"Fresh heads on spikes trouble you?" Beck chastised himself silently. He hadn't meant to say it harshly. Not that Evan would notice. Evan had a blind spot for social nuance. His mind was narrowly tuned to his intellectual interests, focused on his numbers.

Evan stopped and turned to look at the head of a spiked boy they were passing.

Beck halted to wait.

Evan took a step closer to the pole, entranced by the agony-twisted face, the evidence of an unclean neck cut. Cords of flesh and tendon dangled out of the throat and swayed with the breeze, and several chunks of flesh stuck to the spike.

For a moment, Beck wondered if Evan was going to reach up and touch the boy's face.

Instead, Evan said, "I'm not troubled, except to think that the number of dead is unnecessarily large. Do you know how many villages lie outside the three towns?"

"Twenty-seven," Beck answered.

"Yes, twenty-seven named villages."

"Named?" Beck asked.

"Small, unsanctioned settlements exist on the frontier," said Evan. "Some even exist between the villages closer in to Brighton. Sometimes they are but a single brave family living for themselves. Others are several families, a dozen or two people." Evan gestured at the long row of heads on the spikes. It looked like he was counting them. After a pause, he said, "Fifty-three."

Beck didn't need to be reminded of the number. He'd been required to be there to count the condemned. He'd watched as Blackthorn's men severed the necks of the screaming men, women, and children. He watched as the soldiers jammed the bleeding heads on spikes, while he bit back his anger over the pointless brutality.

It was another in a long line of episodes that reinforced Beck's belief that the wrong men were ruling the three towns. Governance, he believed should be in the hands of learned, thinking men, not hypocritical zealots and generals.

Evan asked, "Do you know what the average birth rate is in the three towns and the villages?"

"Three." Beck answered, raising a hand. "We've talked through the complexities of this before so spare me another walk through the details. Can we simply skip to the point you want to get at?"

Evan waved at the line of heads. "Instead of spiking these people, they should have been banished to build a new frontier village. If they survived, in two generations, there'd be two hundred of them, and in four generations, a hundred years from now, it would be larger than any of today's villages."

"If you are trying to construct an argument that would sway General Blackthorn away from spiking people, then you need to understand something. Just as babbling hokum is Father Winthrop's faith, brute force is General Blackthorn's. Neither will be swayed by logic garnered through mathematical methods they do not understand."

Evan's frustration was written on his face. "Could it be explained to Minister Blackthorn that there will come a time when the demon horde returns?"

Beck laughed out loud. "Every child in the three towns knows the stories of the demon hordes that used to sweep out of the ancient city. Those hordes used to come once or twice a generation. We've been lucky to have peace for the last forty years and our people have prospered."

"But Minister Beck, we have no reason to believe that the demons have gone forever."

"No, of course not." Beck furrowed his brow. "Spasksy's Blue Shirts hunt them down in the forests. I venture to guess that they kill several hundred per year."

Evan shook his head. "One thousand, eight hundred and thirty six, on average."

Surprised, Beck searched Evan for some sign of deception. "You collect counts of the number of demons killed each year?"

Evan nodded.

"Why?" Beck asked.

"In death, their numbers have value."

"How so?" Beck asked.

"The number of demons killed goes up nearly every year. Ten years ago, when I started the census, the number was only a few hundred. Now—" Evan raised his eyebrows.

Beck shook his head. "I've seen Blackthorn's men train. He is a tyrant, but he is a superb general. Perhaps his men excel at exterminating them, and are improving each year."

"I subscribe to an alternative explanation."

"Which is?" Beck asked.

Evan paused. "I believe the population of demons increases each year, even though we see relatively few."

"And where are these demons hiding?" Beck asked.

"Perhaps the forest." Evan said, "Until they mass and fall on us like the grasshopper plague. The phenomena are not altogether different. Grasshoppers are always here, and we pay them little mind. But once a decade, they mass into black clouds, rolling over our fields and eating every crop to the nub."

"You think the demons are like grasshoppers?" Beck wondered why he tolerated Evan sometimes. He could be as irritating as he was brilliant.

"Yes," Evan answered. "I think a horde of demons is growing out there in the forests and in the ancient city. One day it will return and destroy our frontier villages or more."

Beck shrugged. It didn't matter that Evan bolstered his demon fear with his census numbers. There were few people in the townships that didn't nurture that same fear. "What is the point of this discussion?"

"A little more patience, please." Evan said. "Do you know how many people died when the last great demon army swept across the villages?"

Beck shook his head. "I doubt anyone does."

"I've studied the question."

Beck laughed. "How could you study something that happened before our census even existed?"

"I have talked to the old men and women who lived back then. I have asked them about the villages that were razed, and about how large those villages were. I asked about the attacks. I asked about the army. I spent a great deal of time on this analysis, Minister Beck, and I believe my numbers are correct."

Beck frowned. Evan was meticulous, even though his methods were unconventional.

Evan said, "I believe that nearly eight thousand people died."

"That number seems high," said Beck.

"I am confident in the number. What I found more disturbing was the death toll in proportion to the population at the time."

"How could you know the population?" Beck asked. Surely, there were limits to what a man could deduce with numbers and questions.

"But from the census, I have learned the birth rate," said Evan. "Using our current population and the current birth rate, which has been stable since I started the census, I was able to work backwards through the math to calculate the population forty years ago."

Beck was taken aback. It made perfect sense. Perhaps Evan was a genius. "I didn't know that could be done."

"I assure you, it can," said Evan.

"How many people were there at the time?"

"Twenty-five thousand."

"One in three died?" Beck's doubts started to rise. "On the last census, you told me there were nearly fifty thousand people in the townships and villages."

"I did. The math predicts the number except for a discrepancy."

Beck smirked. "Your math was wrong?"

"I thought so at first." Evan smiled.

"Please, get to the point."

Evan gestured at the heads on the spike. "If you count all of the people that General Blackthorn spiked for their offenses, calculate the number of their children, and now their children, you will find the discrepancy."

Beck sighed. "How large of a discrepancy are we talking about?"

"Thirteen thousand."

That number surprised Beck. "He put thirteen thousand people to the spike?"

Evan shook his head. "Not directly, but that's how many fewer humans are alive today because of Blackthorn and his spike. Spiked people can't reproduce, and non-existent children can't have children."

Beck frowned at the cost of Blackthorn's brutality.

"My fear is that when the horde comes again there may not be enough of us to survive the attacks and we will go the way of the Ancients."

Beck started to walk. They crossed half the plaza in silence when Beck said, "Perhaps General Blackthorn is worse for Brighton than even I suspected."

Evan stopped and slowly shook his head. "This long-term effect of spiking is bad, but—"

Beck waited for the rest of the sentence. "Speak."

With reluctance, Evan said, "I have been tracking other numbers."

"Yes?" Beck asked.

"The spiking is not the worst problem we face. There is another. If my data is correct, demons or not, we are all going to die."

Chapter 20: Ella

The sky was a tangle of crimsons and oranges when Ella, William, and Bray reached the base of Wanderer's peak. After a full day of hiking, the three travelers had fallen into a rhythm—Bray in the lead, Ella and William tight behind him, as if they'd practiced the formation for weeks. It'd been half an afternoon since their last stop and Ella's legs were sore, but she knew they needed to press on.

The dying light was like a fourth companion, keeping them on track and pushing them along.

For most of the afternoon, they'd been unable to see the mountain through the thick forest, but now that Ella had a clear view, the sight was breathtaking. She stared up the steep slope. The side was flecked with trees, but about halfway up, the landscape gave way to stone and shrubs. The mountain's peak seemed miles away, and she was reminded of some of the stories the townspeople told of the ruins—buildings whose tops seemed to extend into the heavens.

It was then that she realized something.

She'd seen this mountain before, on her way from Davenport to Brighton to become Ethan's bride. The sight hit her with a wave of nostalgia, and her eyes watered. She looked over at William. His mouth hung open, and his eyes danced around the steep slope.

Bray stopped them with an upturned hand, and she was wrenched from her memory. "If we run into anyone, I'll do the talking," he said.

Ella and William nodded.

Bray resumed hiking, navigating the slope with practiced ease. Ella and William struggled to keep up. As they made their ascent, Ella listened for noises from other travelers—some sign that they weren't alone—but heard only the gleeful chirps of birds. Aside from the three demons and the deer they'd encountered the day before, their journey had been quiet, and Ella was grateful. More human contact would lead to more questions, and questions would lead to getting caught.

Bray remained quiet. The setting sun seemed to have dampened his mood, and Ella understood his sentiment. Out in the wild, there were no barriers to separate men from monster, and loss of visibility often meant loss of life. They'd been lucky to pass the previous night safely in the Ancient room. She hoped they'd have similar luck at Wanderer's Peak.

They passed out of the trees as green vegetation gave way to roots and rocks. Ella mimicked the moves of the experienced man ahead of them. She saw several paths worn into the side of the mountain, but she noticed Bray was skirting around them, as if he was trying to elude some unseen enemy. The rapid ascension had her breathless, and she fought the urge to stop and rest. She could still hear Bray's words in her head.

A lot of townsfolk aren't used to the exercise.

Even a day later, the comment still bothered her, and Ella felt the need to prove her worth. She pushed harder. She glanced behind her, peering at the wall of trees that they'd left behind, thinking she'd hear shouts in the distance. But the landscape remained quiet and still.

She'd just taken another step when William stumbled on a pile of loose gravel, and his hand slipped from hers.

"Wait!" she hissed to Bray.

The Warden paused and turned. His eyes were dark and piercing, and he scoured the trees behind them, his hand on his scabbard. William was breathing fiercely. Ella rubbed his back. Evidently, he was as winded as she. For a second, she had the nervous feeling that his condition was a result of his sickness.

But that couldn't be possible.

She'd seen the unclean in town, and their limbs had been strong. Even when they were brought to the pyre, their muscles stretched and shook as they fought against the ropes.

"I'm okay," William said, as if reading her mind.

He wriggled from her grasp and resumed the climb, as if he had something to prove to himself. Bray nodded and turned back to the mountain. Ella picked up the rear.

As their altitude increased, Bray's path continued to wind, and soon they were traveling sideways, battling against the rocky ground. The sun sank lower, obscuring their view, and Ella strained to see. Although she'd passed by the mountain in her journey twelve years ago, she'd never climbed it. They'd stayed in the settlement villages.

If her trip had been planned, Ella would've arranged similar accommodations.

But there was no way she could've known William was infected, no way she could've known about the guards. No way she could've predicted any of this, least of all planned for it.

She was so wrapped up in her thoughts that she almost didn't notice that Bray had stopped in front of them. He halted them with a gesture, his body tense. She clung to her knife.

What is it? She didn't dare speak the question out loud.

Two large outcroppings had sprung up in front of them, jutting out from the side of the slope. Bray was staring at the larger of the two. It took Ella a second to determine what he was looking at.

There was someone underneath it.

She caught a glimpse of clothing, then the outline of a face. A person was sitting upright, resting against one of the rocks. The three of them remained still. Waiting. After a few seconds, she heard the rhythmic sound of the person breathing. She felt Bray's hand on her arm. He put his finger to his lips, urging silence, and the three of them continued up the slope.

When they'd gained some distance, he leaned over and whispered in her ear.

"That was a Warden. There'll probably be more resting up ahead, so stay quiet."

She nodded, hoping that the fading light masked the fear in her eyes.

Chapter 21: Ella

They passed several more Wardens on the way. Each time, Bray led Ella and William silently past them, keeping a buffer zone from the Wardens makeshift camps. At one point, a Warden sat upright and called out to them, but Bray quietly announced himself, defusing a confrontation.

They were more than halfway up the mountain when Bray stopped again. The sun had disappeared, and the world was grainy and unclear. Bray was little more than an outline, his features indiscernible. He raised his hand and pointed at a jagged rock that protruded from the side of the mountain.

"We'll rest here," he said.

"Why here?" Ella asked

Bray didn't answer. She furrowed her brow as Bray scurried toward the rock. She watched as he traced the side with his hands, feeling his way around the edges, and suddenly he was gone, as if the darkness had swallowed him up.

Was it some sort of cave?

A minute passed. Ella's panic grew as she glanced around the mountainside. What if Bray chose to leave them? For almost an entire day, she and William had been at the Warden's side, trusting his guidance, and he was gone. She grabbed William's arm, keeping him close while she waited for Bray to reappear.

Ella and William remained still. The sounds of daytime had been replaced by newer, foreign sounds — sounds Ella couldn't identify, and she found herself glancing every which direction, trying to pinpoint the sources.

After another minute, Ella took a step toward the rock. William followed. She reached out and touched the outcropping, running her hands along the edge, trying to decipher where Bray had gone. She followed the contour of the stone until she'd found a small opening. She quickly retracted her hand.

"Bray?" she hissed.

No answer.

Had something happened to him?

"Bray?" she repeated.

Her words echoed and died, as if she were nothing more than a specter, and the words she whispered were those of a ghost. There was no response from the dark hole. She envisioned Bray crawling through the cave, making his way toward some hidden exit, laughing as he left them behind. Was this some sort of trick? Had he ushered them up the mountain just to abandon them? Why wouldn't he have abandoned them at the Ancient room?

The longer she waited, the more Ella was certain that he'd left, and her fear turned to anger. She should've known better than to trust him. He was just a Skin-Seller, after all. She'd been warned about his ilk. And yet she'd followed him like a child.

What a fool she'd been.

Ella turned around, and was ready to collect her son and find safety, when a voice sprang from the darkness.

"Ella? It's safe. Come on in."

She hesitated, still in the throes of anger. When she looked back at William, she could hardly see his face.

"Let's go," she whispered.

She and William dropped to hands and knees, their elbows and knees scraping against the floor of the cave. Ella couldn't see anything in front of her, but every once in a while she heard Bray's hushed voice guiding her onward. The first ten feet were narrow, but suddenly the cave opened up, and she was able to straighten her back and lift her head.

"That's far enough," Bray said.

She felt around in the black and found William's arm. He startled as she took hold of it. She glanced back in the direction from which they'd come, but could see only a pinprick of light in the distance. The cave reeked of animal urine.

"I can't see, Mom."

"It'll be okay."

Ella settled into place. She grabbed hold of her son and held him tight against her. The cave was cold. Her arms goose bumped, and she felt drafts coming from unseen places. Even though it was early autumn, it felt like the cave had preserved the last remains of the dead winter before.

"Why didn't you answer us?" Ella asked.

"I'm sorry. I was checking the other side. There's another opening letting out about ten feet further along the mountain. I had to make sure no one else had gotten in. Don't worry — we should be safe."

"It's cold in here."

"There's not much I can do," Bray explained. "It's too confined an area to risk a fire tonight. Besides, someone might see the light shining from the cave entrance."

"Do the other Wardens know about this cave?" Ella asked.

"I don't think so. I've never seen anyone else here, and I've been careful not to share the location."

"How'd you find it?"

"My father showed me." Bray went quiet. He rubbed his hands together, and she heard him adjust his pack. A minute later, he stretched out on the floor. "We're going to be here a while," he said into the darkness. "So you might want to close your eyes and pretend you're back at home."

Ella remained in a sitting position, her mind aflutter. Ever since she'd left Brighton, she'd been unable to relax, and she doubted she'd be able to relax now. Even her night in the ancient room had been restless. But at least there they'd had a fire. She heard the scuff of boots and hands next to her. William removed his pack, but he didn't lay it down. It sounded like he was waiting for permission. Either that, or his mind was as preoccupied as hers.

"Why don't you get some rest, honey?" she urged.

"Okay."

William took off his pack and dropped it to the floor. He adjusted and laid down. Ella remained upright, listening to the din of insects and animals outside the cave. Although she didn't like their situation, it was better than being out there. She held her breath for seconds at a time, trying to convince herself that nothing was crawling in after them, that no one had seen them enter. After several minutes of silence, she finally laid down.

Ella held her hands up in front of her eyes, but could see nothing — not a shape, not an outline. The walls and the ceiling were black. Even in her darkest dreams, there'd always been some measure of illumination. If it weren't for the nervous breath of her son beside her, she'd have been certain she was in Hell.

She didn't know what Hell was like, exactly. She'd heard Father Winthrop's stories and rhetoric, but she'd never been able to get a clear vision. Could anything be worse than a town that burned its citizens alive? A town where even the thickest of blood was betrayed? Even on her happiest days, Ella had always lived under a cloud of fear, a sobering knowledge that everything she had could be taken away in an instant.

Losing Ethan had proven that. And now they'd want William.

But all that is behind you now. You've made it out.

She tried hard to convince herself, but found little comfort.

Still cold, she held her arms to her chest and did her best to keep warm. She'd packed a few blankets, but she hadn't thought she'd need them. Not this soon. Winter was still months away. She could hear the thin breathing of William beside her.

"Do you need a blanket, William?"

The boy paused. "Yes."

Ella shifted in the darkness, locating the drawstring on her bag. She loosened it by memory, untangling the knot she'd tied. She dug through her belongings and pulled out a thin blanket. The fabric felt strange in her hands. It'd been her aunt's. She'd never envisioned using it in a place like this. She handed it to William. Bray shifted from somewhere beside them.

"Bray?" William asked, after a pause.

"Yeah?"

"How'd your father find this place?"

"My father was a wise man. He knew lots of things others didn't."

"Was he a Warden?"

"Yes. He was like me, only stronger. I have no doubt he sold two thousand scalps in his lifetime."

"Really?"

"Yes. He was well revered in the wild."

"What was his name?"

"Edward Atkins. But everyone called him Fuller. He was the toughest man I've ever known. If he hadn't taught me the way he did, I would've died a long time ago."

"Why'd they call him Fuller and not Edward?"

Bray cleared his throat. "According to legend, he was fighting a band of demons by himself, close to the mountains, when his sword snapped. Most men would've run. But not my father. Rather than flee, he fought the entire swarm with a broken blade, and he didn't stop until he'd defeated them."

"How many did he kill?"

"Eight of them."

"With only half a weapon?"

"Yes."

"So why do they call him Fuller?"

"The Fuller is the middle of the blade, between the point and the shoulder. That's where his sword snapped, according to the tale."

"How'd he do it? How'd he defeat them?"

"My father never spoke of it. The only way we knew was because of the blacksmith. He told the town after my father brought the sword in to be melted down. Word quickly spread. For years, my father wouldn't respond to the nickname, but he finally gave in. Fuller was a tough man, but he was also humble."

"Is he still alive?"

Bray went silent for a second. "Not anymore."

"Did the demons get him?"

"William!" Ella warned. "That's not polite."

"It's okay," Bray said, clearing his throat. "He died in combat. He was part of Blackthorn's army during the Great War."

Ella's heart thumped.

"Blackthorn? General Blackthorn from Brighton?"

"Yes, but not the Blackthorn you know. Blackthorn's father. Fuller was promised a small fortune to join the man's army, and he agreed so that he could provide a better life for us. Unfortunately, he never came home."

"I'm sorry to hear that," William said, regret in his voice.

"There's nothing to be sorry about. My father died with honor. That's more than I can say for a lot of people nowadays."

The cave went silent, filled only with the subtle chatter of insects outside. Ella heard the scuff of a boot, then the sound of her son turning over. She could tell William was getting tired.

"My father was brave, too," he said, after a pause.

"Was he a soldier?" Bray asked.

"No. He was a farmer. But he was a great man, and everyone respected him. They were all upset when he was taken to the pyre."

"He was infected?"

"Yes, but he turned himself in. He was a courageous man. The only thing he cared about was that we were safe."

"He certainly sounds brave," Bray agreed.

"He was."

William stifled a yawn, and Ella reached over and fixed his blankets. "Why don't you get some rest, honey?" she coaxed.

"Okay, I'll try," he said.

Within a few seconds, she heard the soft sounds of William sleeping. Ella lay awake for a while longer, contemplating the things her son had said about Ethan.

William was right. Ethan had been brave, and up until the end, all he'd thought of was his family.

She held onto that thought as she drifted off to sleep.

Chapter 22: Minister Beck

Beck sat at the ancient table, alone. According to Blackthorn family legend, it was salvaged from some ancient building when The People numbered less than five hundred. The table was intricately constructed with various wood grains and colors, and the edges were cut in beautifully pleasing curves. The feet were carved into animals' ornate legs that curved up to support the massive table, and each side seated a dozen. Beck knew of no such piece of furniture ever having been made in Brighton. The legend had to be true.

At the moment, it was just Beck and Evan.

The door to the kitchen opened, and through it came a woman with a single glass of water on a tray. It was an actual glass, not a carved, wooden cup that stank of all the soaked-in soup grease and wines it had once held. Beck knew from dinners and celebrations in Blackthorn's dining room that Blackthorn had enough glasses to set one in front of every man at a full table. Such was the opulence of Blackthorn's home.

Beck knew that many merchants were wealthy enough to own glass cups, and even porcelain plates, but few had matched sets, and fewer still could feed two dozen with matching pieces.

The girl sat the glass in front of Beck. "I can bring you a snack while you wait on the others, if you'd like."

Beck smiled. "No. That won't be necessary."

With a nod, she pointed to a little silver bell halfway across the table. "If you need anything, just ring."

"Of course." Beck had been here enough times that he didn't need that instruction. The girl must be new. He smiled at her again and she walked back to the kitchen.

A moment later, Father Winthrop arrived with his novice, Franklin, in tow. "Good evening, Minister Beck."

"Hello." Beck smirked. It was an immature game that angered Winthrop and amused Beck. Every man needed his simple indulgences.

Franklin scooted the chair out for Winthrop, waited until Winthrop got comfortable at the table, and took his place against the wall behind him.

Winthrop treated his novices like women, in Beck's opinion. That was a shame.

Another girl came out of the kitchen with a plate of berries and sliced apples. She sat the plate on the table between Winthrop and Beck. "General Blackthorn will be here in a moment."

"Thank you, girl," said Winthrop.

Beck smiled and imagined what she might look like under that dress.

Once the girl had gone back into the kitchen, Winthrop said, "If you'd marry, you wouldn't have to ogle every pleasant-faced woman you see, and spend your evenings touching yourself."

Well, it was certainly starting early this evening. "If only I had the practiced hands of a novice to touch it for me," Beck answered with a wry smile.

Winthrop turned red and Franklin stifled a giggle.

Blackthorn entered the room, with two armed men following close behind. Franklin's giggle stopped. The men took up positions against the wall behind the head of the table. Blackthorn crossed the room in silence, gave Beck and

Winthrop a curt nod, and sat at the head of the table. He reached over and selected a slice of apple. "Eat, gentlemen."

Beck and Winthrop each took a piece of fruit.

"Beck, you said you had urgent matters to talk about at this meeting. Why don't you start?" Blackthorn crunched the green apple slice.

Beck swallowed a strawberry and said, "All of you are aware of the work that Scholar Evan has been doing with the census."

"A waste of time," Winthrop muttered.

"So you say." Beck reached out and scooted the plate of fruit closer to Winthrop. "Please, Father, have more berries."

Winthrop glared at Beck, but didn't take any.

Beck turned to Blackthorn. "What we hoped to learn from the counting, as you might recall, is how to manage our food supply. Since the times of the Fifty-Seven, ration management has been critical to the survival of The People."

"The farmers have always provided," Winthrop said, with a dismissive wave of his hand.

"In our lifetimes, yes," Beck said, "but not always. We've heard stories about the famines of old."

The table remained silent.

Having captured their attention, Beck continued. "Through a variety of analytical processes—"

"Spare us your meaningless words." Winthrop smiled wickedly. "We all know you're smart, Beck. That's why you're the minister of learning."

Beck was unfazed. "Our population is growing faster than at any time in the past."

"How can you know?" Winthrop asked.

Beck looked at Winthrop innocently, thanking the stars Evan had provided him with the fodder he could use to humiliate Winthrop. "Analytical processes."

Behind Winthrop, Franklin failed to completely suppress a smile. Beck would have to talk with Evan about that boy. The boy didn't appear to be completely enthralled by Winthrop, despite the years he'd spent as the man's novice. Maybe he could be of use to Beck.

"Continue, please." Blackthorn was irritated early. Usually it wasn't until the main course arrived that he lost his patience.

"As you all know, the winters have been longer these past few years," said Beck.

Winthrop huffed and leaned back in his chair with a handful of berries. "I thought we were talking about how many people your odd Scholar Evan had counted."

"Enough." Blackthorn pounded the table. That was exceptionally early. Beck wondered what else might be going on that he wasn't aware of. Perhaps Beck would have to snoop around and find out.

Beck looked at Winthrop. "Father, seven of the last ten winters have been longer than usual. The day of the first freeze arrives sooner each year. The date of the last snow comes later. What's more, the springs and summers have been drier in six of those years. This has been particularly pronounced in the past five years."

Blackthorn crunched another apple slice.

"The People do gorge themselves when the weather is good," Beck conceded. "But The People also preserve food. They dry fruits, vegetables, and meats. They store grains and nuts. When times are good, their stores grow. When times are bad, their stores shrink, as do the stocks in the townships' storehouses. When winters are long, the farmers cannot feed their pigs, goats, and sheep because they don't have enough grain. They don't have enough to feed themselves. So they kill some of the animals to feed their families and stretch their hay, so that the remaining animals will live through the winter. But when they kill too many animals, they have fewer baby animals in the spring. Fewer baby animals means less meat and less goat's milk during the summer and the next winter."

Trying his best to seem bored, Winthrop said, "When the weather is better, the farm animals do well and have more offspring. Natural cycles. That is what we're talking about here, right?"

"No, it is more than that," Beck said. "Weather variations are natural, of course. The history that my weathermen keep shows that we have cycles of five to ten years in which the winters are colder and the summers are dryer. Those harsh cycles are offset by periods of five or ten years when the winters and summers are mild."

"Then these cold winters are past us." Winthrop dusted his hands together to dramatize his point. "Good riddance."

"It may not matter," said Beck.

"How so?" asked Blackthorn.

"Our people live on a diet of grains, vegetables, meats, and dairy. They need to eat all four to get enough food to stay alive. If there are no meats and no dairy, the grains and vegetables alone will not be enough to keep them fed through the summer, let alone the winter."

"Not a problem. We have plenty of goats, pigs, and sheep. I stepped in at least two piles of sheep dung on the way here." Winthrop looked around, as if hoping to solicit a laugh.

Beck shook his head at Winthrop. The loquacious dullard. "By consuming so many of the animals over the past few winters, we don't have enough left to produce offspring."

"Then we grow more grains and vegetables," Blackthorn concluded.

"It would seem that easy," Beck answered, "But it takes work to prepare a field, whether it be for grain or for vegetables. The farmers can only prepare after they have tended their regular crops. Under the best of conditions, it is unlikely we could prepare enough land for planting in time to avert a famine."

"What are you trying to say?" Blackthorn asked.

"If we have unfavorable weather conditions, the famine will come this winter or next."

The door to the kitchen opened, revealing a woman with a tray of meat large enough to feed a dozen men. She was followed by two more carrying roasted potatoes and vegetables.

Chapter 23: Bray

Bray waited until Ella and William were asleep, then crept to his feet. He'd kept his bag packed and his sword within reach, and he collected both of them, placing them on the ground near the back entrance.

He paused, taking in the silence.

Outside, he heard the chirps and chatter of night animals. For years they'd been his only companions. Bray wasn't used to sleeping with others nearby. He much preferred the company of his sword and his knife. At the same time, he knew a good opportunity when he saw one, and Ella and her boy were easy targets. He could've robbed them last night in the ancient room, but the firelight had swayed him. At least here it was dark.

He crept over to Ella first. Of the two bags, he was pretty sure hers contained silver. He'd seen her hiding something when they'd stopped to rest the day before. The clink of metal might as well have been the cry of a wounded animal, and it drew him like a hungered beast. He hovered above the woman for several seconds, listening to the soft sounds of her inhaling and exhaling, then hunkered down next to her head. He grazed the side of the bag until his fingers located the drawstring. It'd be difficult getting into it—especially with Ella using it as a headrest—but he'd give it a shot.

He loosened the knots with nimble fingers, encountering no snags, and then parted the folds. He waited. Ella was still entrenched in sleep. He doubted he'd wake her. The panic and unease of the day were better than a stomach full of snowberry. Given what the woman had been through, she'd probably sleep until morning.

By that time, Bray would be gone.

He snuck a breath and dug into her bag. His fingers snagged on a piece of clothing, and Ella groaned, shifting her head. To his delight, Ella's movement had exposed more of the bag. He crept past several layers of clothing, feeling around the bottom, and found the small pouch he'd seen her hide earlier. He pulled it out and pocketed the silver.

He searched for anything else of value. Other than garments and berries, there wasn't much. He pulled out the food and laid it on the ground next to him. He'd take the berries. There was a chance he could sell the clothes and blankets, but he wouldn't bother with them.

Her knife, on the other hand—now that would sell for a few bits to a Davenport merchant.

He reached over her sleeping body. She'd tucked the blade beneath her, and he snaked it out from under her arm. Once he'd secured his take, he retied the bag.

That would confuse her—just for fun.

He brought the stolen goods over to his bag and slipped them inside. Once he'd packed, he returned to the boy. William was out cold—his breath was slow and even. Bray had low expectations for the contents of the boy's bag. Chances were he'd find only clothing. But he'd check all the same.

He hated to leave easy pickings.

He crouched next to the boy, tracing the ground until he'd discovered the edge of the bag. Even in the darkness, Bray knew his way around. He practically lived in this cave in the winter. He regretted showing it to the pair, but he wasn't worried. Without him guiding them the rest of the way to Davenport, they'd probably die in the forest.

Bray untied the boy's bag and wormed his hand inside. The boy took a deep breath, and he waited for him to exhale.

Clothes. Clothes. More clothes.

Finally he hit on a few pouches of berries, and he carefully slid them out. He was about to conclude when he felt something metal. He removed the object and rolled it in his hands, furrowing his brow. It was some sort of figurine. Whatever it was, he could probably sell it to the merchants. Even if it weren't valuable, they'd melt it down. He tucked it in his pocket.

He was just retying the bag when a whimper escaped into the darkness. William's head rolled to the side, knocking into Bray's hand. He felt a hard knot against his fingertips, and he darted backward.

Was that—?

Bray froze. He stared into the darkness, wondering if he'd been imagining things, but the sleeping boy provided no answers. He considered creeping back over, double-checking the boy's neck, but he knew what he'd felt.

The mark of the monster. Evidence of the unclean.

In an instant, everything became clear. He'd known Ella and William were fleeing from something, but he'd been certain they were debt-runners. He hadn't suspected this. Did the woman have a lump of her own? He scampered away from the sleeping duo, bringing the boy's belongings with him. He could turn the pair in, but there wouldn't be any money in that. He'd be thanked for his service and sent on his way.

He crept to his bag, packed it up with his newfound goods, and slung it on his shoulder. He snuck out into the night.

***

Bray was halfway down the mountain when he saw torches in the distance. He ducked down and surveyed the bobbing lights. Despite the apparent activity, the forest was quiet. It'd been a while since he'd seen a hunting party in these woods, and rarely did he see one at night.

Had Brighton sent a search party for Ella and the boy?

Although it was clear that the pair were on the run, he didn't think the town would send out several of its troops at night—especially not for an infected mother and her son. The wild was hardly a place for humans in the darkness. Besides, torches were a bad idea; the light would just as easily draw the demons as it would flush out the people they were trying to catch. Idiots. Bray shrugged, resolved to continue. A minute later he stopped.

There was a chance he could score something from the troops. At the very least, he could eavesdrop on their conversation.

He scooted down the mountain. The light of the moon was hardly enough to illuminate the landscape, trees or not, but it was better than nothing.

Going downhill was much easier than going up, and before long, he was creeping through the trees, his knife drawn. As he scouted forward, he strained his ears for sounds of the men. He heard voices, subtle murmurs in the distance. He kept moving toward them, doing his best to avoid detection. The relationship between soldiers and Wardens was tenuous. Neither liked each other, but each was protected by the same law. Although they often argued, they rarely got violent. Any bloodshed would come before Blackthorn.

That was a consequence no one wanted to face.

Bray cast aside bushes and bramble, closing the gap. In the event the soldiers heard him, he'd announce his presence to avoid being attacked, but he'd rather it not come to that. It looked like the lights in the distance had stopped.

He drew within a hundred yards and paused next to the trunk of a large tree. He peered around, catching sight of the group. As he'd suspected, the lights belonged to soldiers. There were four of them. They loitered in a circle, conversing. They looked young and inexperienced—they'd probably volunteered for the night hunt to curry favor with Blackthorn. One of them, a man with a chiseled face, had captured the attention of the others. He was on a rant, his eyes darting from forest to fire as he spoke.

"I swear I'm going to gut her myself," the soldier spat.

"Easy, Rodrigo," said one of his companions.

"If we weren't bound by the laws, I'd cut off her arms and feed them to the demons while she watched."

"You know you can't do that."

"She killed my cousins!" Rodrigo began pacing back and forth. Rather than being calmed by his comrade, he grew more irate. "When I find her and that boy, I'm going to—"

Was he talking about Ella?

Another soldier grabbed Rodrigo's arm. "You'll do nothing!" His face was bearded, and he looked slightly older than the rest. "Do you want to answer to Blackthorn? Because I don't. If you touch her, Goddammit, I'll have your head on a spike myself. She's to be brought back as an example. You know that. We all know that."

"Did you see the goddamn bodies? Did you see what she did to them?" Rodrigo asked.

"She'll answer for that, rest assured."

Rodrigo's eyes blazed, but he fell silent.

"Two days and no luck," said the third soldier. "Where do you think they went? Do you think the demons got them?"

"I don't know," the bearded man said. "Even if she knew where she was going, we'd probably have run into her by now."

"I bet she's holed up in one of the caves on the peak. Maybe she found her way into some Skin-Seller's filthy den," the fourth soldier chimed in.

Everyone laughed, except Rodrigo.

"Did the other group already go out?"

"They probably passed us. They were crossing the river."

The soldiers fell silent. Bray waited patiently. They were eating and drinking, taking a break from the chase. After the last man had finished, they wiped their faces and picked up their torches.

"Let's split up," the bearded man said. "Two of us will tackle the base of the mountain, the other two will climb the peak."

"I'll take the peak," Rodrigo growled. "Maybe I can get something out of one of those filthy Skin-Sellers."

Brandishing torches and swords, the soldiers forged back into the woods.

***

Bray skirted back into the underbrush, trying to stay ahead of the group. Branches whipped against his face and trees seemed to appear in front of him, but he held up his knife to try and ward off nature's attack. He thought about what he'd heard.

Although the soldiers hadn't used Ella's or William's names, it was obvious who they were looking for. The possibility that there were more than one woman and child on the run was remote. By the sounds of it, Ella had killed several Brighton soldiers.

They'd probably forced themselves on her.

The story was a familiar one. Although the soldiers had rules to follow, they often used their power to their own ends. Rodrigo was one of the worst ones. Bray could see it in the man's body language.

The man would torture Ella, if he found her.

Not my problem, Bray thought. He had wares to sell.

His bag bounced on his shoulders as he ran, and he envisioned the items inside. He'd had a productive day. An extra skin, some silver, and some belongings he could sell. It wasn't enough to retire into one of the finer houses in Davenport or Coventry, but it was more than what he'd woken up with.

He skirted around the base of the mountain, intending to avoid the woman and child he'd left behind. Bray was ready to head toward Davenport. He wasn't keen on traveling at night, but he was anxious to get his silver.

If all went well, he'd never run into the soldiers he'd seen.

He didn't need the complication.

As he ran, he counted in his mind the money he'd receive in Davenport: five each for the skins, and five for the knife. That'd be enough to survive for at least a week, if he were frugal. And if he didn't encounter any other monsters on the way. If so, that would mean even more coin.

Bray smiled.

He felt a surge of excitement in his bones—the thrill of a man in the wild, providing for his own needs. It was a sensation he'd grown addicted to over the course of his life; the moment he lived for.

His father had instilled that feeling in him, back when he'd first taken him into the wild. Bray had been only six years old then. He still remembered the first monster he killed. His father had wounded it, and he'd allowed his son to finish it off. That was how his father had taught him how to skin. It was a memory that Bray had held onto ever since, and one he looked back on when things seemed bleak, or when silver was scarce.

The memory warmed him now. He darted between the dark outlines of trees, smiling. Out of nowhere, he remembered the figurine in his pocket.

He'd almost forgotten about it.

He patted his pants, ensuring it was still there. He wondered what had possessed the boy to bring it. It must've had sentimental value.

Whatever it was, the boy wouldn't need it much longer, anyway. The boy was infected. His life was a walking death sentence. Soon, his body would fill with sickness and delusion, and eventually, he'd become one of them.

Another scalp for Bray to skin.

But Bray would wait until the boy had turned.

He pictured the boy's body, littered with knots and warts, and then he pictured the boy holding the figurine. Out of nowhere, he felt a pang of guilt.

Stop it. Bray tried to dismiss the image, but it persisted.

He recalled the words the child had spoken before he'd gone to sleep. The fond memories he had of his father, the genuine curiosity he'd had for Bray's endeavors. Did the boy know the end was near?

If so, why did he go on?

Then he thought about what Rodrigo had said about Ella.

I'm going to gut her myself.

The soldier would probably do the same to the boy. Bray felt a sick feeling in his stomach. Before he realized his actions, he was turning around and heading back to the cave. He shouldn't have left them behind. Infected or not, no one deserved to die like that.

He leapt up the base of the mountain, dashing as fast as his legs would carry him. He needed to make sure Ella and William stayed hidden.

He just hoped he'd make it in time.

Chapter 24: Minister Beck

After the meeting ended, Beck sat in his room staring into the fire, dwelling on his foul mood as the night passed. It had been another in a long series of wasted meetings. The Council of Elders was a misnomer at best, a joke at worst. There was no council of three. There was only Blackthorn and his servile fool, Winthrop. Beck was an intelligent observer whose efforts were continually thwarted on anything but the most trivial of matters.

Some day in the future—maybe soon, maybe some years from now—the price for Brighton's dysfunctional government would need to be paid. The empty-bellied people and the dying children would blame the Elders. That was how the peasants always reacted when hunger set in and snow covered the ground.

They'd beg. They'd point accusing fingers at one another. They'd rob. Eventually, they'd look at one another's gaunt faces and realize the merchants were not thin. They'd see that the soldiers had been well fed. They'd see no sallow cheeks among the Elders. And they'd point their bony fingers away from one another and at those with full bellies, those in positions of authority.

Once the fingers started their pointing, there'd be no way to avoid the rioting. The merchants' houses would be looted first. The soldiers would try to stop it, to preserve order. That would pit the soldiers against the peasants and solidify the two sides in the coming anarchy. On one side would be the starving, powerless nobodies, the ones who did what they were told, who lived in hovels, farmed the fields, and burned on the pyres. The other side would be the well-fed, with horses, swords, and spears, who lived in warm barracks or opulent houses and did the telling at the point of a sword.

But peasants would lose their fear of swords when their children were starving. Though most farmers couldn't count the toes on their feet, it wouldn't take much mathematical aptitude to figure out that their mob would greatly outnumber the men with swords and the fat merchants and town Elders they were protecting.

It would start in one town and spread to the others. Riot would turn to revolution. The soldiers who didn't flee in the chaos would die, clubbed to death with farm tools. Beck would burn on the pyre, with Blackthorn and Winthrop at his side, not for having a wart or a smudge, but for the sin of having too much meat on his bones.

When it was done, the people would eat what the wealthy had hoarded. When that food was gone, the peasants would continue starving. The children would be the first to die. And a starving man would eat anything he could get his hands on, even his neighbor's children.

It wouldn't be the end of humanity, just a reset. There'd be many fewer people in the townships when spring finally arrived. The survivors would forage in the forests and grow food in the gardens and fields. There'd be no livestock by then. The slow process of domestication would have to start over.

In the last famine revolt—an event only whispered about among the old people—it was estimated that only one in ten people lived. That had been two hundred years ago.

One in ten. What a disaster that would be.

The bestial demons were the wild card, though. More than a generation had passed since the last of the great hordes fell on the villages and towns. If they came back again in the numbers and frequencies told in stories, man's reign on the great flat earth would come to its end.

And that's what brought Beck to contemplate the most drastic action of all. Should he take enough of his scholars and women—fifty-seven, ideally—and preemptively flee? Should he go somewhere far away from the ruined, demon-infested cities, and start a new civilization, a civilization where knowledge was placed above superstition and sword?

Could that be done?

Or was the solution more obvious? Was the better solution to supplant superstition and the sword right here in Brighton?

A coup?

A heavy knock on the door startled Beck out of his thoughts. Dread slithered through his seditious bones. Nobody pounded with such impunity on the door of a minister so late at night. Nobody but Blackthorn or his soldiers. Dread faded into despair as Beck sensed what the knocking represented. Just as he was coming to the conclusion that action needed to be taken, all choice was to be taken away from him. Beck slumped in his chair.

The pounding came again. Louder this time.

Weakly, he said, "Enter."

The door swung wide and a soldier strode in as if he were coming into his own apartment. "Minister Beck?"

"Yes."

"Minister Blackthorn requires your presence."

Requires? "I dined with him earlier this evening. Is it possible that you are late in following your orders? Be gone and let me have my sleep."

"I left Minister Blackthorn's presence and walked directly here. I am not late." The soldier looked down at Beck and waited.

Beck glanced at the door, spotting the outlines of several other soldiers there. Perhaps he'd argued vehemently for his view one too many times. He only hoped he'd have the choice to take the sword.

On joints and bones that suddenly felt old and creaky, Beck stood. He looked around the room for an excuse to take him out of the soldier's hard gaze, to buy him some time to think of a way out. But there was none. There was only the pyre.

Beck motioned to the door, a silent request for the soldier to lead the way.

"After you." The words were those of courtesy, but the tone made it clear that Beck had no choice in the matter. On the way through the door, Beck took his overcoat and wrapped it over his shoulders.

Three other soldiers were in the hall. They arranged themselves around Beck, two in front, two in back, and clomped their way down the stairs. At the bottom were a half dozen of Beck's scholars, standing silently in the great room, watching the soldiers take their master into the night. Beck saw the fear on their faces. It was the same fear he had in his own heart.

He shouldn't have let his passions run away with him during dinner. He shouldn't have berated Winthrop for his superstitions with such a vitriolic tongue. More importantly, he shouldn't have shamed Blackthorn for his inability to grasp the obviousness of the coming crisis. Powerful men don't accept such slights without plotting revenge.

As the soldiers led Beck through the town, he remembered his father, his predecessor on the council. He had disappeared in the night when Beck was a young man. The next day, he'd found his father's bones tied to a burned pole above the ashes of a smoking pyre.

When Beck went to Blackthorn for answers, Blackthorn explained that Beck's father had come to him in the night, distressed over a growth of wart he'd found on his head. Blackthorn begged Beck's father to wait until the next Cleansing to come forward, but Beck's father had insisted in dealing with the problem straight away, lest he infect some innocent farmer or barren woman.

And so Beck's father insisted on mounting the pyre that very evening.

Beck still remembered Blackthorn's telling of the story. Blackthorn looked at the ground while he spoke. He seemed genuinely sad to have lost a long-time colleague and friend. And Beck, apprehensive though he was, believed Blackthorn, because believing was so much easier than not. Not believing brought with it all kinds of moral imperatives that Beck was not willing to face. Because facing them meant prevailing or dying.

Beck was not a fan of dying.

The five walked across the square. Beck was sure that he'd soon be adding his burning smell to the stench of pyre ash and rotten spiked heads.

Behind and to the left of the dais stood Blackthorn's massive home. It was the de facto seat of government in the townships, the place where every decision was made. The guards stopped at the door and knocked. It opened immediately. Of course, they were expected.

Beck had been sent for.

The soldiers walked Beck through the wide door, two abreast. Beck appraised the door and decided it would be impossible to defend when the famine came. Blackthorn's burnt stench would waft over the plaza soon enough.

Once inside, Beck was guided back to the place at the table where he'd sat arguing through the course of most of the evening. A few minutes later, Blackthorn came in with three of his captains. "Beck," he said as they all sat down, "explain to my officers what you explained to us earlier this evening."

Beck looked at the intricate designs on the table. "I understood from our conversation earlier this evening that a decision had been made."

"Don't be a fool, Beck." Blackthorn's voice was harsh. "Winthrop needs to be humored to keep his simple ego intact. No decision was made. Tell us what you and your scholars understand about the coming famine."

Beck looked up suddenly. Maybe he'd live.

Maybe there was hope for the townships, after all.

Chapter 25: Ella

When Ella awoke, the world was dark. Her heart was thudding from the remnants of a nightmare, but even the world of her nightmares had light and color. This place was pitch black.

It took her a few seconds to realize she was still in the cave. She drew a breath and stared around, hoping for a glimmer of light. The details leading up to this minute came spilling back to her. She recalled the escape from Brighton, the altercation at the river, and their journeys with the Warden. Then she remembered William's fond words about Ethan as he'd drifted to sleep.

She must've joined him in sleep shortly afterward.

She explored the ground beside her, reaching out to her son. But there was no one there. Frantic, she snapped awake and crept to her haunches, exploring the damp ground. All she found were pebbles and dirt and his blanket and bag. She kept searching, her heart beating at a nervous gallop, until she finally stumbled on a person.

William was still there. He was asleep. He must've rolled out of his blanket. She sat up and expelled the thick, anxious breath she'd been holding. Her muscles ached, as if she'd spent an afternoon pulling grain in a cart race. Her head throbbed. She crouched and reached above her. She still had a foot of clearance from the ceiling. Something stirred in the darkness, and she heard the flap of wings. Ella stifled a scream as something flitted past her and out of the cave's opening.

Bats.

That explained the smell of urine. She waited a moment, then stretched as far as she was able, wiggling her arms and legs to restore the circulation. Although the cave had saved them from danger, it was starting to make her feel claustrophobic, and at the moment, she felt the overwhelming urge to get out. She crept forward, feeling her way with her hands. She saw a pinprick of light at the entrance—a small cluster of stars deep in the night sky. She wanted so badly to go outside and breathe the air, if only for a minute.

But that'd be unwise. Other Wardens might hear her, and she might give away Bray's hiding place. Besides, she couldn't leave William behind.

Instead, she stopped moving and fell silent, listening to the sound of William breathing. Despite everything they'd been through, he was still alive—alive and with her. The fact that they'd made it this far was encouraging.

Maybe there's hope.

She took in the stars for a few moments, then worked her way backward, retracing her steps to her bag. Her stomach was growling. For the past days, they'd hardly eaten, other than the few berries they'd consumed. She knelt to the floor and located her pack, then untied the knot, searching for food.

But when she reached inside, past her clothing, she found nothing. What the hell? She kept searching, thinking that any second she'd feel the rough texture of a skin, or the soft leather of her silver pouch. But all she felt was fabric.

Something wasn't right.

The food pouches were gone. And so was her silver.

She must have missed them; they had to be here. She tore through her bag, removing the items and casting them aside in the dark, her panic mounting. Soon the bag was empty and her belongings were piled up next to her. But there was no sign of any food or silver. Her belongings had been stolen. And the only person who could've taken them was…

"Bray?" she hissed into the dark.

She waited for a response, already knowing she wouldn't receive one. She felt dread creeping up her spine like a slithering snake. Receiving no answer, she called out for her son. She heard him beginning to rouse.

She should've trusted her instincts. She shouldn't have fallen asleep. Instead, she'd made the mistake of letting this man lead them up here, only to rob and abandon them.

"Mom?"

Her son sounded groggy—the same way she'd felt when she'd awoken several minutes earlier.

"I'm here, honey," she said.

She caressed his arm, feeling vulnerable and stupid and angry. This shouldn't have happened. Not only had Bray stripped them of their food and silver, but he'd also taken the knife. They had no way to eat. No way to protect themselves. No way to buy anything when they got to Davenport.

She felt the rage building up inside her like water behind a dam, begging for release. Not only had Bray stolen from, stranded, and condemned her, but he'd done it to William as well. She silently vowed revenge. She gritted her teeth, wanting nothing more than to scream obscenities into the dark, to beat on the walls and hunt him down. The only thing stopping her was the threat of compromising their hideaway.

They were trapped until morning. And even then, Ella didn't know how they'd survive the journey to Davenport. As she'd learned at the river, legs alone wouldn't save them from the monsters. The creatures were quick and vile. Encounters with them were inevitable. And if they weren't prepared, Ella and William would draw their last breaths in the wild.

Powerless and ashamed, Ella buried her head in her hands and cried quietly, doing her best to hide the sobs from William. Soon he'd ask questions, and soon she'd have to answer them. He'd want to know why Bray had betrayed them. William would want to know how someone posing as a friend could do such a thing.

And she'd have no idea what to say.

"Is it morning?" William asked.

She heard him shifting on the ground, searching for a hint of light.

"No, it's nighttime, honey. I'm sorry I woke you. I just wanted to make sure you were okay. Go back to sleep."

"Is Bray still here?"

Ella fell silent. She didn't want to do this. Not now.

"No, honey."

"Where'd he go?"

"I'm not sure."

"Is he coming back?"

Ella swallowed the lump in her throat. "I don't think so."

The boy fell silent. This time she was unable to hide her tears. Although William was young, he was perceptive, and he'd discover the truth anyway. She heard him sit upright, and a moment later, she heard him digging through his bag.

"What are you doing?"

"Looking for something," he said simply.

"What are you looking for?"

"Zander."

She frowned in the dark, unsure of what he was talking about. "Who's Zander?"

The boy stopped digging. She could sense that he was embarrassed, though she couldn't see his face.

"My figurine," he replied, after a hesitation.

"The one from Dad?"

"Yes. I brought him with me. He's not here. Did Bray take him?"

She heard him digging again, growing more frantic by the second, each nervous breath like a needle to her heart.

"Yes. He took some of our things, honey. He took our things and then he left." The tears were flowing now, and Ella could barely get the words out. "He's not an honest man, William."

"But I thought he had a good man's heart of stone. I thought he was like Dad."

William cried out and flung the bag to a distant corner of the cave. His voice cracked and quivered. She grabbed onto him and held him tight.

"I'm sorry, honey," she whispered. "I'm so sorry this happened."

Chapter 26: Bray

Bray raced back up the steep slope. Torches moved along a trail in the darkness below. He'd put some distance between himself and the men—they weren't as familiar with the area, so they'd be moving more cautiously.

That would give him time to get to the cave.

He scrambled among the rocks and stone, setting a few of them rolling, and winced at the noise. The last thing he needed was to draw the men's attention. It'd be enough trouble hiding the woman and the boy as it was.

Before long he'd approached the jagged outcropping that marked the entrance. He saw the outline by the dim light of the sky. He ducked behind the rock, wedging himself through the entrance. All at once, he was inside, breathing hard and heavy. He heard noises from deeper in the cave, and he crawled toward them. Were Ella and William awake? Had he disturbed them?

"It's me," he whispered. "It's Bray."

The sounds ceased.

All at once his cheek erupted in pain. Bray threw up his hands to defend himself, readying his knife. Ella's voice raged through the darkness.

"You son of a bitch!" she yelled.

He scooted backward, trying to avoid the woman's blows. He had to restrain himself from lunging with the knife.

"Quiet!" he hissed.

"You took everything we had. Why are you back? Did you forget to take our blankets?" she cried. "My food and my silver weren't enough for you?"

"I wasn't—"

Another blow stung his face, and this time he whipped his hand forward and caught Ella by the wrist. He pulled her close, until her hot breath was against his skin. She writhed against his grasp.

"There're soldiers out there! They're coming for you!"

"You son of a bitch! I hate you!"

"Ella! Stop!"

This time he raised his volume, imparting his concern. Ella stopped struggling, suddenly grasping the meaning of his words, and they both went silent and still. In the distance, he heard the commotion of men. It sounded like the soldiers had run into another of the Wardens, and were interrogating him somewhere down the mountainside.

"Listen," Bray whispered. "Do you hear those voices? Those are soldiers from Brighton. They've come to take you back for your crimes."

"My crimes?" Ella spat. "My crimes? What about yours? What about robbing us and leaving us to die?"

The woman was nearly hysterical, and it took all Bray's efforts to calm her down.

"Let's discuss this later, Ella. Right now, we need to stay quiet. I know you hate me, but if you both want to live, you need to listen."

He let go of the woman, hoping the gesture itself would win back her trust. There was no time to argue. He spun back to the entrance, focused on the men outside. He heard the sound of raised voices, then the clank of swords. It sounded like the other Warden had been drinking, and in his inebriated state, the man had started an argument with them. That might work to their benefit.

Perhaps the other Warden would distract the soldiers. Maybe he'd even kill them.

If Bray were alone, he would've used the cover of the commotion to leave, but with Ella and the boy at his side, he didn't think it'd be wise. Not in the dark.

Ella crept up next to him. Her arm brushed his, and he could feel her still shaking.

"You have no conscience," she hissed in his ear. "I should've killed you in your sleep. I should've done it when you came through that entrance."

"I'm glad you didn't," he whispered back.

"You're no kind of man."

Bray shook off the insult. He'd heard worse.

"I could've turned you in," he said. "Do you know that? I still might. Maybe I'll get a reward."

"But I've done nothing wrong," she whispered.

"Do you think that matters?"

"The soldiers in Brighton tried to rape me. They were going to hurt William—"

"I don't doubt it."

"I'm not like you, Bray. I haven't killed for pleasure; I've killed because I had to."

"I know." He grabbed her and put his mouth to her ear. "I know why you did what you did. I know about William."

That was enough to stifle Ella. They hung in silence for several minutes, listening to the clash of men down the mountainside. Finally, Ella spoke.

"What do we do?" she whispered.

"We stay put."

"What if they find us?"

"They won't."

"But—"

"If they do, we'll use the other entrance. We'll figure it out."

Ella sat back on her haunches, and William crawled over to join her. The fear in the cave was thick and tangible, and all of a sudden, Bray felt the weight of three lives on his shoulders. For years, he'd wandered the wild alone, beholden to no one. And now, things felt different.

He hadn't created the situation, but for some reason, he felt responsible for fixing it.

"Why don't you two wait further back?" he whispered.

"But—"

"I mean it. Stay behind me."

"Am I going to get Zander back?" William asked.

Bray felt a pang of remorse, and he reached into his pocket and passed back the figurine. He heard the soft scuttle of boots and dirt, and all at once he was alone, staring through the cave's opening.

He kept his knife in front of him, ready to make a move. The fighting from down the mountain had stopped. He heard the tramp of boots on gravel, then silence. Had the other Warden been killed?

He listened intently, hoping for a clue as to what had happened, but heard only the background noise of animals in the forest. It was as if the night had swallowed up the men, relegating them to his memory.

He released the breath he'd been holding.

Ella and William remained silent. Even if the soldiers were gone, the forest wasn't safe. They'd wait until morning, and then all three of them would head to Davenport. Bray would just need to avoid the common road.

His eyes flitted across the stars, as if he were plotting a trip of the heavens rather than planning a trip to Davenport. If all went well, they'd reach town by midday. He'd give Ella and William their belongings back, and then they'd part ways.

More minutes passed.

He'd wait a little longer. If he heard nothing in that time, he'd get some sleep.

The opening of the cave went dark.

Bray's pulse spiked.

He tightened his grip on the knife. Someone was breathing heavily outside of the cave's entrance, but he could make out nothing of the person's appearance. A voice echoed across the walls of the cave.

"Throw your weapons and come out of there. Don't make us come in after you."

He recognized the speaker.

It was Rodrigo.

Chapter 27: Father Winthrop

Father Winthrop sat in his favorite evening chair, watching the light from the fire reach across the large room and play along the wrinkles in his bed sheets.

He was angry and he was sad.

The image of young Jenny's head on the spike would not leave him alone. Between the Cleansing yesterday, and Blackthorn's putting all of Ella Barrow's friends' heads on spikes today, it was hard to bear so much death. The Cleansing was necessary, of course. But the spiking?

Jenny, eyes glued to Winthrop, had begged him to spare her life in front of half the town, right in the middle of the square. She'd looked at him with those engaging brown eyes, as wisps of her wild, sandy hair blew across her face and clung to the tears on her cheeks. Her wrenching pleas seemed to have been birthed rather than cried, thrust into a ghost realm where they could haunt him over and over. And the ghost of her familiar voice keened above the crackle of the fire in his bedchamber. Imagination? He didn't know. He couldn't tell.

What he did know, what he felt, as solidly real as he felt the hard wood of the chair beneath him, was hate. Not hate for simple-minded Jenny, but for Blackthorn. It was on Blackthorn's whim that the sword came down on the back of her neck, crunching bone and tearing ligaments, squeezing one last attenuated scream from the condemned woman. Those sounds haunted Winthrop, too. They turned his grief into nausea that rose in his chest and burned his throat when he swallowed it back down. Together, it mixed with the guilt in his gut and turned his bowels to water.

Father Winthrop grunted audibly at the cramps in his belly.

If he'd known that cowardly Ella's Barrow's best friend had been a sandy-haired girl from The House of Barren Women, he would've prearranged for Jenny to be elsewhere before Blackthorn's men pulled her to the platform. But Winthrop didn't have that foresight, and for that reason he felt guilt.

Unfortunately, once Jenny had been rounded up and corralled in the square with the rest of Ella's friends and acquaintances, Winthrop had no choice but to ignore her. To brush away the brutal hand of Blackthorn's justice in front of all the town's men and women would be to sow the seeds of anarchy in the minds of the simple peasants. It would give them the false hope that they too could sidestep deserved justice. Anarchy would grow and that would be the death of them all.

Or would it?

That made Father Winthrop wonder. Was it the thick sword arm of a brutal dunce terrorizing the townsfolk that coerced them into obedience, or was it something else? Certainly Blackthorn was the leader of the Council of Elders — though no such position formally existed — so his brand of rigid rules and harsh justice was most visible. But no, Father Winthrop suspected that the foundation of society was not fear, but love of The Word and devotion to it.

Our beliefs. Our god. Those are the threads that hold the fabric of our society together.

Winthrop sat up straight and repeated that epiphany in his head.

Surely that had to be true. Winthrop nodded, letting this conviction sink down to his core.

That epiphany almost made Jenny's death meaningful.

The Council of Elders should not be a military dictator with two impotent figureheads alongside. In fact, it shouldn't be a council at all. As the Bishop of Brighton and head of the church, Father Winthrop was the natural choice for leading the government. Who else would know what was best for the people? Who else knew the divine Word as intimately as he?

Something needed to change. The government needed to change. And as a pillar of the government, Father Winthrop needed to change it. He let those thoughts germinate for a bit while he tried to repress the fear he felt for Blackthorn. In the meantime, he went back to staring at the bed sheets, watching Jenny's head topple from her neck and reliving her haunting scream.

The knock on his door came later than expected, but it was a welcome one, chasing away the memories of the day's brutality. "Enter, boy."

The door latch scraped and Franklin pushed the door open. He squeezed through the small gap he'd made for himself and closed it behind him.

"Tell me about her," Father Winthrop asked.

"She is from The House of Barren Women."

"I should hope so." Father's Winthrop's emotional distress turned to vitriol. "That is where I sent you, is it not?"

Franklin flinched back a step. "I'm sorry, Father."

Winthrop turned to look at the fire. In a tone that belied his words, he said, "You are forgiven. What is her age?"

"Twenty-six at most."

"Did you ask her?"

"Yes Father, but most of those women either don't know or they lie."

Father Winthrop nodded slowly. That was true enough.

"But she looks to be of that age," Franklin added.

"Good." Winthrop turned on the boy. "Two years ago, when Jenny was down with the fever, you brought me a wrinkled crone to take her place. I wonder sometimes if you can tell a young woman from an old one."

Franklin looked at the floor, futilely hiding a smile. "I may not recall correctly, Father, but I understood that you enjoyed your morning with Beverly very much."

"Beverly. Was that her name?"

"Yes, Father."

"I did enjoy my time with her." Winthrop smiled weakly. "That is true."

"If you enjoyed her, why did you not ask me to bring her again?"

"She was not pleasing to my eye. Still, one wonders, with her skill and imagination at bringing a man to pleasure, how she could have remained barren for all the years of her long life."

Franklin meekly said, "Some say the fault may lie with the man."

"I assure you, young Franklin, that no fault lies with me. I spent my seed just as any true man should. I do my duty every time you fetch a barren woman for me."

"My apologies, Father. I didn't mean that."

"Of course." Winthrop's voice softened. "Speak no more of such heresies. Tell me about the girl you brought. If she is a girl of sandy hair and brown eyes, I'll flog you. I have no desire to be reminded of yesterday's atrocity. I wish to forget all my times with Jenny by drowning those memories in the arms of another."

"Her hair is raven black. Her eyes are blue ice. Her skin is milk white."

"And her breasts?"

"Large."

Winthrop nodded approval as he mumbled. "Jenny had small breasts." This woman didn't sound like she looked anything like her. "How long has she been in The House of Barren Women?"

"Two years."

"Good. I have no desire to work through a woman's fear of men. And the woman who runs the place, Mary, what did she say of this girl?"

"Mary assured me that Fitzgerald—"

"Fitzgerald?" Father Winthrop didn't like that name at all. "An odd name for a girl, don't you think?"

"It is the name of one of the first fifty-seven."

"Do you think I do not know that, Franklin?"

"My apologies, Father. I…I don't know why I said that. Would you like me to bring her in?"

"In a moment." Father Winthrop's face turned thoughtful. He appraised Franklin as he recalled his vindictive hate for Blackthorn. A dim hope was brimming in his head, a hope that he might have the strength and cunning in him to make the change in the government that he yearned for. Winthrop asked, "You are good with numbers, is that true?"

"Yes, Father."

"What is the highest number you can count?"

Franklin giggled. "There is no theoretical limit to the numbers that can be counted. Thank you for testing my knowledge with that question, Father."

Father Winthrop snorted. He'd have to ask someone else to find out whether that was true. It couldn't be true though, could it? No limit? That made no sense at all. "You spend too much time in the company of that strange bird, Scholar Evan."

"He has taught me much, Father."

"Good." Winthrop scratched his head and thought about his nascent plans. "I have questions that I want you to find answers for."

"Questions with numbers?" Franklin asked.

"Yes."

"What answers would you like me to find, Father?"

"How many men take their devotion to The Word to heart?"

"All men do, of course," Franklin answered.

"I don't ask how many men sleep through the recital of The Word, young Franklin. Nearly all of the men attend our devotional service. I ask how many men sit in the pew and passionately assimilate every word, longing for the next word in the way a soft-hearted man longs to touch a woman under her skirts."

Franklin said, "Pardon my ignorance in these matters, Father, but may I ask why this number is important?"

"I need to know how many men's devotion to The Word is absolute," said Winthrop.

"This may not be an easy answer to find," said Franklin. "It may not be a matter of simply counting. How soon will you need this number?"

"I know that it may be hard to find this answer. Consult with Scholar Evan. Perhaps he has knowledge of these things through the census that he runs each year. We'll talk more about this in a fortnight. Tell me at that time what you know."

"I will." Franklin gestured to the closed door behind him. "Would you like me to let her in now?"

"Yes. I'm tired of talking and thinking."

Chapter 28: Bray

Bray sat silent in the cave, listening to the demands of the men outside. Someone must've heard him. Someone must've seen him enter. He gritted his teeth. He sensed Ella and William behind him, huddled in a corner.

"Get the hell out here, now!" Rodrigo yelled.

It sounded like the man's rage was increasing by the second. Bray could probably spring from the cave and slash the man's throat, but there was at least another soldier with him. As confident as Bray could be, he wasn't careless, and he wasn't stupid.

He crept backward on hands and knees, keeping his eye on the darkened entrance. Soon, he was crouched next to Ella and William. He felt for Ella's arm, drew her close, and hissed in her ear.

"I'll check the other exit. Hold still."

He gave one last look at the dark entrance, then turned and made his way to the other side of the cave. As he crawled, he held onto his scabbarded sword, trying to distill any noise it might make. It didn't take long to determine that the other exit was compromised.

The soldiers had them walled in on both ends. It looked like there were three—two at the main entrance and one at the other. He wasn't sure where the fourth had gone. He returned to Ella and William and gave them strict, whispered instructions to hug the wall, then took out Ella's knife and pressed it back into her hand. He made for the original entrance.

The soldiers conversed loudly. One of them talked about coming in. Another insisted tossing in a torch and burning them out.

"Wait a moment!" Bray yelled. "I'm coming. Can't a man get some sleep?"

"Throw your sword and come out slowly!" Rodrigo yelled. By the sounds of it, he was in no mood for jesting.

Rodrigo stepped away from the entrance, revealing the glow of several torches outside. The light permeated the cave, bouncing off the walls, and Bray had the sudden, panicked thought that Ella and William were about to be exposed. He continued crawling, trying to block the light and capture the men's focus. When he'd reached the entrance, he unsheathed his sword—a difficult task, considering he was in the cave's mouth—and tossed it in front of him.

There were three soldiers at the main entrance. The one from the back had already joined the others. Bray's eyes darted from Rodrigo to his two companions, taking them in. The fourth—the one with the beard—was missing. Bray glanced instinctively down the mountainside, as if he'd catch a glimpse of him, but saw only the dim outlines of stones and mountain shrubs. It was possible the inebriated Warden had killed him. Either that or Rodrigo had.

Rodrigo's face was yellow and hardened. He bent down and retrieved Bray's sword, grinning. A second later, one of the others walked over and held a blade under Bray's chin.

"Is that any way to treat a protector of the settlements?" Bray asked.

"Shut up, Skin-Seller. Come out the rest of the way. If you make any sudden movements, I'll slit your throat," the soldier warned.

"Relax. I was just trying to sleep."

Bray climbed out of the cavern. He attempted to stand, but the soldier kept the blade at his throat and prompted him to stay on his knees. Bray's anger rose. He envisioned thrusting a knife into the man's neck, watching him spill blood onto the side of the mountain.

But not yet. Not while he was outnumbered.

Rodrigo bent down, coming to within inches of Bray's face. His cheeks were flecked with wet blood. His breath stank of woodland squirrel.

"Hopefully, you'll be as uncooperative as the last one." Rodrigo grinned wickedly.

His eyes effused the same madness Bray had seen before, but this time the madness was amplified, fueled by confrontation and violence.

"Aren't you breaking the pact between Wardens and Soldiers?" Bray reminded him. "Unless you have proof of some wrongdoing, I haven't done anything to warrant this treatment."

"To hell with the code," Rodrigo spat.

"Even out in the wild, there are rules. You know that. Aren't you from Brighton? Blackthorn must've taught you that."

At the sound of the General's name, Rodrigo backed up a step and lowered his sword. The soldier next to him followed his lead. The one with the knife to Bray's neck remained in place.

"I'll answer your questions," Bray said. "But I'll do it on my feet."

Rodrigo gave a reluctant nod, and the third soldier lifted the blade from Bray's neck. All at once, Bray was free. He bent down, making a show of getting to his feet.

"Now, how can I help you?"

"We're looking for a woman and a boy," Rodrigo said.

"A woman and a boy? In the wild?"

"Yes. They're infected, and they killed two soldiers back in Brighton while fleeing The Cleansing."

"A woman and a boy wouldn't last long out here," Bray said, making it so obvious that even the dim-witted, angry Rodrigo might conclude the same. "Did you search for remains?"

Rodrigo didn't bite. "There're no remains. We know they had help."

"It's possible, but I haven't come across them."

Rodrigo glared at him, and Bray noticed the two other soldiers eyeing the cave's entrance. He held his position, doing his best to appear cooperative, but blocking their view.

"If they passed through this area, I probably would've seen them. I've been out hunting all day."

"They're infected," Rodrigo reiterated, giving him a sideways glance. "They're dangerous."

"Like I said, I haven't laid eyes on them."

The other two soldiers scowled in silence.

"What are you doing here, anyway?" one of the other ones asked.

"Sleeping. What's it look like? I'm on my way to Davenport."

"What do you have in the cave?"

"My bag and belongings."

"We'll need to check. Then we'll be on our way."

Before he could protest, the soldiers moved to push him away from the entrance, torches held high. Rodrigo remained in place, locking eyes with him. He was still holding Bray's sword. It felt like Rodrigo was daring him to make a move.

The man's eyes were like coals.

Bray kept his eyes locked with Rodrigo, reaching for the knife he had tucked in the back of his pants.

Bray sprang at Rodrigo.

Chapter 29: Ella

Ella listened to Bray and the soldiers talking outside the cave, her pulse climbing. She held William in her arms, waiting for the inevitable to occur—for the soldiers to find them—to be forced to fight.

On Bray's instructions, they'd crawled as far from the entrances as possible, doing their best to stay concealed in the cave's darkness. Even then, she knew hiding was no guarantee of safety. If the men were to come inside, surely they'd find her and William.

She listened to the soldiers outside speak about the escapees from Brighton. The words sounded strange, as if the events had transpired to people she'd never known, in some place far away. It was hard to believe what her life had become. In just two days, her living space, her profession, and her safety had been stripped from her, all because of a society that would rather kill than listen.

She couldn't go back there. Wouldn't go back there. And neither would William.

The soldier's harsh young voice came to an unexpected stop. Bray had made his case, apparently hoping to convince the soldiers the cave was empty, but they'd insisted on seeing for themselves. The torches grew brighter in the cave entrance, and Ella closed her eyes, as if she could make herself invisible. They'd almost made it undetected. They'd come so far…

Someone cried out from beyond the cave's entrance, and all at once the torches withdrew. She heard the bustle of commotion, cries of pain, and shouts of men.

"Come on!" she hissed to William.

The cocoon of shadows would protect them no more. She flexed her elbows and knees as she stood, gripping her knife and clenching her jaw. The time for cowering was over. The time for bravery had arrived. She pulled at her son's arm. Then she grabbed their bags and slung them on. Before she knew it, they were panting and crawling, heading for the second entrance. They'd have to run and evade the men, but at least they'd be moving.

Her dress bunched up beneath her, and her knees stung from the scraping of skin on stone, but soon, they were at the opening, peering out into a star-filled night. The men had dropped their torches, and light blazed from the ground. Several illuminated figures clashed with swords. She recognized Bray's form in the fire glow, his face hard and determined. He swung at one of the soldiers, sending the man screaming to the ground. Ella tumbled out into the open, pulled her son from the cave, and started off down the rock-covered slope.

Gravel spit from beneath them, threatening their footing, as if the mountain itself were bent on impeding their escape. Ella held tight to William with one hand. She gripped the knife in the other, dinging it against the rocks and dirt as she rushed down the slope.

"Over here!" one of the soldiers cried.

She and William were out of the pool of light thrown by the torches, and she could barely make out the terrain in the darkness, but she pressed on. She dug her heels into the ground, praying she'd stay on her feet, praying the mountain wouldn't topple her. But the loose rocks kept shifting.

The rocks beneath her had become a mini-landslide, rolling and tumbling, the roar of stone and gravel drowning out the other sounds around her. Ella tried to find purchase, but she twisted her ankle on a stone. Suddenly, Ella was falling, pitching headfirst down the mountain. She let go of

William's hand so she wouldn't drag him down with her. She flung her elbows in front of her face as she landed. The impact was hard and sudden, knocking the wind from her stomach and rattling her insides. The bags flew off her shoulders. She continued sliding for several feet, and all of the sudden she was at rest, loose rocks rolling around her. William skidded to a stop nearby.

"Mom! Are you all right?"

"I'm okay," she managed, through a mouthful of dirt.

"Someone's coming!" His voice was frantic.

She struggled to get to her feet, but she was lying headfirst on a slope. It was difficult to get traction. William grabbed her arm to help her. She could barely see him in the dark.

"Mom! Hurry!"

She was on one knee, still getting her balance, when a body collided with hers. William's fingers ripped free. Ella sprawled back to the ground. A man had tackled her. She tried to scream, but her lungs were stripped of air and she could barely breathe.

"Stay still, or I'll cut you open! I'll do it in front of the boy!"

She recognized the voice as the man she'd heard outside the cave, the one who'd been interrogating Bray. She writhed and squirmed. It wasn't until she felt the cold steel of a blade on the back of her neck that she stopped moving.

"That's better," he hissed.

She couldn't see the man's features, but she sensed an aura of venom around him. It was the same malice she'd felt at the hands of the soldiers in Brighton, the same hateful expectation that bled from a crowd of spectators right before someone got burned. She might've escaped Brighton, but she was in less of a position to do so now, in the dirt and on her stomach, weaponless and in the dark.

"Let the boy go," she tried, but her plea died in the dusty rocks.

A hand grabbed her by the hair. Rather than pulling her to her feet, the soldier dug the blade deeper into her throat. She felt a sting, the wet sensation of blood trickling down her neck.

The soldier turned to William. "Sit on the ground."

Ella couldn't see her son, but she heard the crunch of boots on gravel, and assumed he'd complied. No, she wanted to scream, but the knife at her neck had paralyzed her tongue. The soldier let go of her hair, swooped it to the side, and groped with abrasively calloused hands along the back of her neck.

"You're not infected?" he asked, surprised.

She remained silent. He pushed her face into the dirt, demanding an answer.

"No," she managed.

"That's a shame, then. But it won't change what you've done." His voice was hollow, soulless. He pressed the knife into her again.

This man wasn't taking her back to Brighton. She could feel it. She would die here on the mountainside. She needed to do something. Anything. She needed more time.

"Do you have children?" she asked, surprised she could still speak. Her body felt useless and tired, as if she'd experienced a dozen deaths already.

"A boy and a girl," he answered, without hesitation.

"What are their names?"

"Shut up, wench! That is no business of yours!"

"But what if they were threatened? Wouldn't you do anything to protect them?"

The soldier remained silent.

"Wouldn't you—?"

"Enough!" the soldier shouted. "You're a murderess! You killed my cousins!"

The man's words were like a punch to the stomach. Ella swallowed, certain she was on her last breath. If this was the end, she needed to warn William. She needed to make sure he ran. Before she could speak, she heard William stand up.

"Sit!" the soldier screamed to him.

The boy remained in place.

"Do you hear me? Sit down, you smudged piece of shit!"

"William, run!" Ella screamed.

All at once, she heard the sound of footfalls on the stone, and the heavy pant of her son as he fled down the mountainside. The soldier kept the knife at her neck, but she could feel his hands shaking with rage.

"Go ahead and run, boy! I'll flay your mother, and then I'll hunt you down and do the same!"

The footsteps waned into the night. Ella swallowed, picturing her son alone and in the wild. There was no way he'd last out there. But at the moment, anything was preferable to what this man would do to him.

The soldier released his knife and grabbed her clothes to spin her over. Ella complied, if for no other reason than to buy her son time. His hot breath dripped in her face, making her repress a gag.

"Are you taking me to town?" she asked, already knowing the answer.

"What do you think?"

"They'll want me to burn for what I've done."

"They'll never know you were found."

Underneath Rodrigo, she squirmed, testing his weight, but he'd pinned her with his knees. He parted her dress, exposing her chest. Ella screamed.

At least I can't see his face, she told herself. At least I can't see what's coming.

"They'll have your head on a spike," she whispered.

"The demons will pick your bones clean, and no one will ever find you."

Ella bucked with everything she had, slipping her hand free, but the man was ready for her, and he grabbed hold of it, squashing her hope before it had a chance to blossom.

With no other option, Ella began to scream. The noise was high-pitched and piercing, and she hated every second of sound that came out of her mouth. Her scream was cut short by the soldier's hand. He pressed his dirty palm against her lips, stifling her.

Then he keeled over, gasping for air.

What the—?

Ella pushed again. This time she was able to wriggle free. She heard the clank of the man's knife as he dropped it on the rocks, and she squirmed out from beneath him, confused. She scrambled clear of his fallen body, listening to the gurgle of his death throes.

A few seconds later, the man was still.

A shadow emerged in the moonlight. She stared at the shaking form.

"William?" she whispered, her lips trembling.

"Is he dead, Mom?"

Chapter 30: Father Winthrop

Father Winthrop looked the girl up and down as she entered his bedchamber. She closed the door behind her and walked a few paces inside. She did indeed have raven hair, milky skin, icy blue eyes, and large breasts that stirred his interest. And that threadbare dress—immodest even for a girl from The House of Barren Women—pushed her breasts up as though they might spill out.

"You are Fitzgerald?" Winthrop asked.

The girl nodded.

As much as Winthrop wanted to see that dress fall away, he had specific preferences in these matters. He liked when they talked for a while before they shed their clothes. "Feel free to speak, girl."

"Yes, Father."

"In these chambers, and nowhere else, you may call me Winthrop. Or if it pleases you, you can come up with some pet name."

Fitzgerald asked, "Do you have just the one name?"

Winthrop snorted. "I don't subscribe to this fashion of labeling oneself with two names. If one name is not memorable enough than what good will two do?"

"Yes, Winthrop."

"Tell me about this name of yours. It is unusual for a girl."

With her hands clasped lazily in front of her, the girl said, "It was my father's. He is able to trace his line all the way back to the fifty-seven."

"I am aware Fitzgerald was one of the first fifty-seven." Winthrop chastised himself for the harsh way he said it. It always irritated him when it was implied — however slightly — that there was something of The People's history that he did not know.

"Please forgive me, Father Winthrop."

"It is nothing. Have you any brothers or sisters?" asked Winthrop.

"I am the only child. I had two older brothers, but they both died during infancy."

Winthrop watched the fire light dance across Fitzgerald's pale skin, glimmering in her glossy hair. She was a beauty. "And your father, presumably also Fitzgerald, had the foresight to save the family name for his third child?"

The girl shook her head. "He named each of the boys Fitzgerald, expecting that each would live. When I was born, my mother died of birthing. Knowing he'd have no more children, he passed his name to me."

"And what does your father do?"

"He cuts wood."

"Did he remarry?"

"No." The girl smiled as though she were putting on a mask. "His heart was broken — or so he told me when I was a young girl."

"Demon, devotion, and seed." Winthrop shook his head as he said it, thinking of his own grief over Jenny's death. "The three duties."

"Slaughter the demons. Be true to The Word. Bring children into the world." The chant was ingrained into every child and the girl spoke it as automatically as if she'd been sitting in the pew. But her smile passed behind a cloud of thought.

Winthrop guessed what had taken away her smile. "Worry not over your father. He sired three children. He did his duty. Luck is not always with a man, though he'd try to make it so."

Fitzgerald nodded and the light of her smile shone again.

"Come closer into the light where I can see you better."

"Yes." The girl crossed the room and stood in front of Winthrop, close enough that he could reach and touch her with the tips of his fingers, close enough that he could smell her. She smelled clean. He preferred women who bathed.

Winthrop looked at the girl's skirt, reached out and ran a few fingers down a pleat. "That dress is in a sad state."

"I don't often have it on long enough that men notice, Father."

Winthrop ignored her use of the word Father. "How long have you been in The House of Barren Women?"

"Two years," she answered.

"Surely your dress is older than that. How could it have become so threadbare in such a short time?"

"Neither my father, nor my husband could afford the cloth for a new dress. This was handed down to me by another." The girl's face turned from seductive to hopeful. "Men sometimes show their gratitude with a coin. In time, I'll be able to buy the cloth for a dress of my own."

Winthrop's eyes showed his anger over the veiled request for money and his voice rose to match. "It is the duty and privilege of the barren women to serve the unwed men of the town. The Word says it must be so. Women who cannot have children will be fed and housed. They do not work the field nor do they tend the flocks. They certainly have no children to look after." Winthrop felt he'd been a little too sharp on that last point. Women's primary purpose in life was to bear children.

But he didn't want the girl frightened of him. That would take all the pleasure out of what was going to occur.

Dispassionately, he said, "Barren women contribute to social stability by putting their legs in the air. It is an easy life and it is a sin for a barren woman to ask for payment. She should keep in mind that the town has generously provided for all of her needs already."

Despite Winthrop's attempt to soften the harshness of his rant, half way through, the girl was nearly in tears. "I beg your forgiveness, Father. I…I was not asking for a gift. I…"

"Speak no more of payments or gifts." Winthrop turned and watched the fire for a short while, ignoring the girl while his anger faded.

The red embers and sparse yellow flames of last nights fire radiated comfortable warmth onto Winthrop's face. The warmth reminded him of Jenny. And thoughts of Jenny hurt. He'd let himself get so attached to her through the years. There were so many good memories, but they were all tarnished with the sound of Jenny's screams, the crunch of her bone, and the vision of her head on a spike.

Damn that Blackthorn and his sadistic fetish for spikes. Could the man's simple mind imagine no other punishment?

Winthrop's heart turned soft and it ached. He was afraid he might shame himself by shedding his tears over Jenny while Fitzgerald looked on. Winthrop closed his eyes and tried to make all the hurt go away.

Eventually, the sound of Fitzgerald's breathing reminded him that she still stood a pace in front of his chair, waiting to do whatever he bade, in order to cleanse Jenny and her haunting scream from his heart.

Winthrop turned to the girl and said, "Remove your dress."

With a hint of hesitation, Fitzgerald reached around to her back and loosed the lace that held her garment closed. The cloth that stretched tautly over her chest loosened and her breasts fell, but not by much. And that was one of the many reasons Winthrop liked the young girls.

Winthrop watched the girl's chest rise and fall with each slow breath. The dress didn't fall away, though. It seemed to drop just a little with each exhalation, letting just enough of the girl's breasts to show that Winthrop thought he could see the edge of an areola. The girl did have a tantalizing way about her.

He said, "You are beautiful."

"Thank you."

"How many men have you been with?"

The girl's face showed a moment of shame before she recaptured her hypnotic smile.

Her shame made Winthrop feel guilty for having asked the question. "I don't inquire in order to shame you, girl. I merely wish to know that you…ah…have sufficient experience in these matters."

Fitzgerald looked at the floor. "Please forgive me, Father, I don't have my numbers."

"You can't count?" Winthrop asked, watching her grow more embarrassed.

She held up her fingers. "I can count as high as my fingers but no more. My father is a woodcutter. He has no such knowledge to teach me. I assure you, I will please you." Feigning a loosening of her dress, the girl put a hand on her breast to keep it from falling further.

Looking at those breasts, Winthrop's doubts disappeared. "I am sure of it."

Chapter 31: Ella

Ella stared at the dead soldier William had slain. Through the moonlight, she could see the handle of her knife protruding from the back of the man's neck. She pulled herself to her feet. Several hundred yards upslope, the faint glow of torches lit the mountain, splashing light on the fallen bodies of the others.

Nothing up there moved.

She approached the soldier her son had killed and grabbed the hilt of her knife. The smell of blood was overbearing, and she covered her mouth to reduce the stench. She steadied herself, then tugged, listening to the sickening sound of metal separating from flesh.

She retrieved the dead soldier's knife and handed it to William. He took it in silence. Since killing the soldier, he'd hardly spoken a word.

"It's okay, honey," she whispered.

William didn't answer. She grabbed hold of him, squeezing him tight.

"Did I really…? Is he…?"

"It's over now, William. It wasn't your fault."

She stared back up at the flickering torches on the mountainside, trying to determine their next move. The soldiers were dead. And by the looks of it, so was Bray. For a moment, she convinced herself that she didn't care about the Warden. He'd betrayed their trust. He'd robbed them and left them to die.

But he'd also come back to save them. She felt a shimmer of sorrow.

She started back up the hill, bringing William at her side. After some searching, they were able to locate the bags they'd dropped. Thankfully, the flaps were still closed and the possessions were still inside. But Bray still had her food and her silver.

She walked up the remainder of the hill, approaching the torch-lit scene. With each step, she made out more details of the slain soldiers in the dark. Their mouths hung agape, their eyes stared into the night. Bray lay beside them on his stomach, a blood-soaked sword at his side. His pack still hung on his shoulders.

She crept over to him. Dead or not, he had her possessions. She reached for his bag. His head was turned in the opposite direction; his hair was caked with blood. Without him, they wouldn't have gotten this far.

They would've died at the river.

William stood several feet away, watching her. She caught a glimpse of his eyes in the torch's glow. She could still see the fright in them, but there was something else, too. It looked like he was in shock.

There was no time to worry over it. She turned her attention back to the bag and eased it off Bray's shoulders, then slung it onto her arm. She'd take the whole thing. He wouldn't need it now, anyway.

When she'd finished, she scavenged the dead soldiers. None of them had any silver, but they had some food and water. She laid claim to all of it and stuck it in her bag. Then she picked up one of the soldier's swords.

She'd never used one before. She hefted it in the air, examining the sword by the firelight. If she wanted to survive, she'd better learn how. She pried a sheath from one of the dead soldiers and put it on.

The torches flickered. After a few seconds, one of them went out, pitching the hillside into semi-darkness.

"Where are we going to go, Mom?" William asked, breaking the silence.

"I'm not sure."

Ella hadn't thought that far ahead. With her adrenaline flowing, all she'd thought to do was to reclaim her possessions. She glanced down the mountainside. The forest was thick and menacing, as if it hosted a single mass of living things. They couldn't go out there. Not tonight.

"Let's go back to the cave," she said.

"Okay," William said, but she could sense his fear.

She wasn't keen on the idea, but at the moment, she couldn't think of a better plan. It was still dark, after all, and the forest wasn't safe. They walked back up the incline. They'd only taken a few steps when a groan whispered out over the rocks from behind them. Ella paused, her heart skipping a beat.

She swiveled. The three bodies near them remained motionless. Rodrigo was out of sight, but she was sure he was dead. Her eyes flitted between the soldiers and Bray. She waited for what felt like an eternity, thinking she was imagining things, but she couldn't be: William had heard it, too. He was stock-still, listening as intently as she was.

Somewhere in the distance, an animal cried, but the moan didn't repeat. She'd been certain the men were dead. She contemplated pulling the sword, but clutched her knife instead. After a minute of silence, she took a step toward the nearest dead soldier. In the absence of one of the torches, his face hung in shadow, but she could see the outline of his features. Nothing seemed to have changed.

The groan came again. This time she pinpointed the source.

It was coming from Bray.

"Wait here," she hissed at William.

She stepped closer to the fallen man, maneuvering until she could see his face. The Warden's eyes had opened.

"Bray?"

He parted his lips, letting out another moan. A stripe of blood ran from his temple to his chin. Ella remained in place for a moment, unsure of what to do, when she heard a crackle from down the mountainside.

"What was that?" William asked, his eyes darting down the slope.

Ella followed his gaze. Something was making its way through the forest. Not just one thing, but multiple things. The forest came alive with crunches — sticks and brush being trampled by footsteps. Demons. Ella backed up a step, glancing back at the cave.

"Are we going to leave him?" William asked, incredulous.

"No," she answered. "We can't do that. We need to move him. Help me!"

Ella grabbed Bray under the armpit, then directed William to take his other arm. The man seemed semi-conscious. They were fifteen feet from the opening of the cave — a short distance, without a body to pull. Ella tugged and strained, but could barely move him.

"Pull harder!" she urged William.

William strained. The noises from down the mountain were getting closer. It sounded like they'd transitioned from the forest to the rocky part of the slope. The Warden slid a few inches, moving toward the cave, but they were fighting against the incline and the weight of his body. Bray groaned softly. Ella wasn't sure how injured he was, but one thing was clear: if they didn't get to the cave soon, they'd all be eaten alive.

"Hold on," she whispered. Ella gritted her teeth, bracing herself on the mountain, and instructed William to pull again.

This time they were able to move the man, and they began dragging him over rocks and stone.

The footsteps hastened. The demons were gaining ground.

Ella tugged with all her might, ignoring the aches and pains of her battered body, sliding the Warden up the slope. Before she knew it, they'd reached the mouth of the cave. She heard inhuman grunts wafting up the mountain, the rattle of loose stones.

Bray moaned louder, as if to spur them on. Ella and William slid him into the cave. There was barely enough room for Ella and William to fit next to each other, but somehow they managed. When they'd gotten inside, Ella stared nervously at the entrance.

The remaining torch outside was still lit. What if the light exposed the cave's opening? What if the demons looked inside? She had the sudden, frantic thought that she needed to douse it.

"Wait here!" she whispered.

She crawled on hands and knees to the entrance and burst into the open. Her dress blew behind her. When she reached the torch, she began rolling it on the rocks and stone, but the flames continued to burn. The noises on the mountainside were closer—a march of the damned coming to take her. She changed tactics, stamping the torch with her boots. If she couldn't put the damn thing out, she'd have to leave it burning.

The things were getting closer.

Finally the torch went out, releasing a cloud of smoke, and Ella darted back to the cave. She scampered through the opening and toward William, positioning herself next to

Bray's motionless figure. She could hear the boy's unsteady breath.

She peered at the entrance. With the torch extinguished, the opening revealed little of the world outside. But she could hear noises—grunts and growls that were no more than thirty feet away. The demons had reached the dead soldiers. She clutched onto William, fear ramming her chest like a stake. Although she couldn't see the demons, she could envision them feeling their way around, exploring the scene outside. She held her breath, as if the mere exhalation of air would alert them. After a few moments, she heard the rabid tearing of flesh, then the sounds of slurping and gorging, sounds that were worse than any nightmare she'd had.

She covered her son's ears and prayed. Though she wasn't sure what God she believed in, anything was better than listening to this. No higher power could condone this savagery.

The feasting lasted for a nearly unbearable amount of time. Each crunch of teeth against bone made her skin prickle. It was as if the soldiers' entrails were her own, their flesh, her flesh.

It was hard to fathom that the demons had once been human, too.

Bray let out a quiet moan, and Ella clamped her hand over his mouth, dampening the sound. The creatures paused in their feeding. After a few seconds of listening, they resumed.

When the last limb had been cracked and the final bones had been licked clean, the demons continued up the mountainside. She listened to their footsteps recede, her breaths still violent and uneven. Soon, the wind blew across the landscape again, as if the world itself had deemed it safe to exhale.

***

Ella didn't remember falling asleep. When she awoke, there was a triangle of light on the cave floor and William was cradled in her arms. The boy was still clutching the knife she'd given him.

She studied her surroundings. Having arrived in the dark, she'd barely noticed the color of the walls and ceiling. The cave was comprised of a deep, dark stone, and she found herself thinking it was beautiful, unlike anything she'd ever seen. Her eyes wandered. She almost jumped when she found Bray staring at her. The Warden was leaning against the far wall, his face caked with blood. His features were barely recognizable. He was sipping a flask of water, and he greeted her when she made eye contact.

"Good morning."

He smiled nonchalantly, as if they'd awakened in a Brighton house instead of a dank hole in the earth. It looked like he'd been waiting for her to arise.

"How're you feeling?" she asked, momentarily forgetting the anger of the night before.

"One of them did a number on my head." He tilted his skull to prove it, displaying the gash in the side of his temple. "So I've been better."

"I thought you were dead."

"So did I. Considering I was up against three soldiers, I did pretty damn well," he mused.

She scanned the rest of his body, expecting to find him wounded, but he was surprisingly intact. "Well, I'm glad you're alive."

"Are you sure? That's not what you said last night."

Ella ignored the statement and looked down at William, who was starting to stir. The boy's eyes fluttered open. After a brief pause, he sat upright, his eyes roving the room.

"It's all right, honey. The demons are gone," Ella assured him.

The boy continued looking, as if he didn't believe her, then sat up on his haunches and stared at the entrance.

"I wouldn't go out there, if I were you," Bray said. "It's a mess. The demons are good at feeding, but they aren't so good at cleaning up after themselves."

Ella grabbed William's shoulder, as if to reinforce the Warden's words. "Stay here, William."

William settled down.

"You must've had a hell of a time dragging me in here," Bray said.

"We managed."

"I owe you one."

His eyes wandered to his bag, which was lying next to Ella. Ella recalled taking it from him the night before, and felt a surge of panic. Bray was staring at her intently. Before she could explain, he cut her off.

"It's okay. You can keep what's inside," he said. "You saved my life. You deserve it."

"Even the demon skins?" William asked.

"Even the demon skins."

Ella unpacked Bray's bag, taking the silver, skins and berries, and tossed the bag back to him. She started to collect her things. "Well, we'd better be on our way. I'm glad you survived."

She slung her bag over her shoulder. With the knowledge that Bray had lived, some of the anger of the previous night returned, and she dismissed her guilt at accepting his things. She started making for the exit, retrieving her sword.

"Do you even know how to use that thing?" Bray asked, frowning.

"I'll figure it out."

"It'll be heavy at first. You might want to take a few practice swings."

Ella ignored him and kept crawling.

"I assume you know the way to Davenport?"

"We'll follow the river."

"That wouldn't be wise, remember?" Bray called. "The river is the worst place to linger."

"We'll stick to the woods."

"I know a safer way."

Ella sighed. "Why don't you just tell us where it is, then?"

Bray took a long sip from his flask. He smiled, relishing the knowledge he held over them. Ella's anger mounted.

"Tell us which way to go, then," she demanded.

"Why don't I just take you there? I can get you there in half the time it'll take you to find your way without me."

"I'd rather go alone."

"I have a few things to take care of in Davenport," Bray said. "Besides, you won't know any of the merchants, and they'll cheat you on the scalps. Then they'll turn a nice profit when they trade them in."

Ella paused, torn between the man who'd helped them and the man who'd betrayed them. If they went with Bray, how could they trust him again? At the same time, heading off alone would be a huge gamble. Besides, they could use his connections with the merchants.

"You'll take us to the fairest one?"

"The fairest, and the best looking." Bray smirked.

Ella rolled her eyes. "Okay. Deal."

Chapter 32: Ivory

At first light, Ivory came to a windswept lip of rock at the top edge of a near-vertical stone face. Somewhere in the past, half the mountain had splintered and fallen away, forming a thousand-foot cliff down to the ground that sloped gently for five or ten miles, to the edge of an endless blue ocean. Breathtakingly tall towers of the old city slowly rusted and rotted on that ground, on both sides of a river, on the small islands offshore, and stretching into the distant gray haze up and down the coast. Brighton was just a speck of a bumpkin village compared to that dead metropolis.

But just as the Ancients who used to live in the old city had disappeared, he knew eventually the remaining towers and smaller buildings would crumble into the forest until nothing remained. Whether it took months or years, decay was inevitable.

At one time, one of the towers had stood taller than the cliff on which Ivory now stood—a vertical living forest, home to a million birds and who could guess what else. Ivory had laid eyes on that building only once, on his first visit to the ancient city. His uncle had taken him there. Some time prior to their next visit, four months later, the tower had collapsed into a mound of debris, burying many of the nearby structures in the vague grid pattern around it.

From atop the cliff, the pile of that giant tower's rubble seemed small, but in fact, it was enormous. Even after its inevitable destruction under the weight of its stones and steel, it stood taller than any building in any of the three towns, and its debris spread wide enough to cover a quarter of Brighton in broken stone. And that was just one of the ancient towers.

On Ivory's previous trip, he'd asked his friend Jingo how many buildings the Ancients had abandoned when they left the old city. Jingo had laughed and asked Ivory to guess. And so Ivory had guessed. But Jingo never answered.

Ivory stood at the top of the cliff in the cold, clear air. It was always the cold days that gave the longest views. He sat on a big rock, close enough to the edge of the cliff that he was able to see most of the ancient city filling the land between the mountains and the shore, and started counting. He'd expected to find the task time-consuming and tedious. He'd also expected it to have an end.

As he counted his way across the grids and odd patterns, the task grew difficult. Some square patterns in the grid contained single structures, some contained multiples, and some seemed to have no pattern at all. There were whole swaths of the city he couldn't see, blocked from view by the ancient towers. Peculiar mounds and hills dotted the old city's patterns—whether crumbled buildings or overgrown forest hills, he couldn't tell. The process of counting, it turned out, wasn't a matter of ticking off units, but a matter of making judgments at each tick.

After several hours, he'd managed to count only a small portion of the buildings in the old city. It'd seemed like such a simple thing when he'd started. As he sat on his rock, staring into the distance, he felt defeated by the task and understood Jingo's laughter. It was impossible to count all of the buildings and houses.

The city had to have been magnificent in those days before the fall, alive with more people that Ivory could imagine, full of inscrutable far-talking devices, flying machines, and terrible weapons of flame, like small bits of the sun brought down from heaven to incinerate the enemy.

Stories of Tech Magic, the secret of the Ancients. Could it have truly been that powerful? Every time Ivory looked at the old city and imagined what it had once been, he believed the old stories. But to believe those old stories was to accept despair. The Ancients had been eradicated by a brutish race of beasts and none of the Ancients' wondrous devices and terrible weapons had saved them.

What did that say for Brighton, with its hovels of wood and stone, its bows and swords, its horses? When would the twisted men finally come to kill them all?

Chapter 33: Ella

Ella, William, and Bray spilled back onto the mountain.

"Don't look, William," Ella warned.

She did her best to shield the boy from the dead soldiers, but she could sense him peering through her fingers. Even in the daylight, the bodies on the mountainside were barely recognizable—carcasses of bone and gnawed skin. Half-eaten limbs were strewn across the landscape, heads separated from spines. Ella shuddered at the knowledge that it'd almost been they who were the dismembered corpses.

Before leaving the cave, Bray warned them to keep quiet. The demons often returned to places where they'd found humans. Not just for days, he'd said, but often for weeks. With that knowledge, they navigated the slope with knives drawn and an eye on their swords. Traveling in the daylight gave Ella some measure of comfort, but it wasn't enough to quell her fear. The demons weren't limited to any particular time of the sun, as she'd learned.

They'd attack anytime.

Soon they'd left the gruesome scene behind. The sun had crested the mountain, and its fervent rays spat upon the landscape, serving as both a guide and hindrance. Ella walked at a brisk pace, trying to keep the sound of her footsteps subdued. William scampered beside her. She noticed Bray was leading them sideways, simultaneously descending the mountain and changing course.

William was scratching his neck. Ever since leaving the cave, he'd seemed distracted and withdrawn, and Ella had done her best to keep him on task. She could only imagine what he was thinking. They'd seen plenty of violence and bloodshed in town, but he'd never killed anyone himself. That must have had some effect on him.

In addition, he was probably afraid of what he was turning into.

The fact that the spores were taking hold of him must be terrifying. As a mother, it terrified her, and it shredded her heartstrings that she couldn't help him. All Ella could do was to buy them some time. Sooner or later, William's delusions would catch up to him, and from then on, his brain would deteriorate.

The knots on his skin would swell and spread.

To be fair, Ella didn't know much about the infection. The stories the townspeople told were often vague and conflicting. Most of the infected people she'd encountered had been on their way to the pyre, ready to burn for sins they hadn't yet committed. She knew what the beginning stages of the infection looked like, and she knew the result, but much of what happened in between was a mystery.

She remembered how Ethan had looked at her before he'd gone to the pyre. His eyes—normally deep and blue—had been shallow and unfocused. It wasn't the look of a man infected, but the look of a man who knew what was coming.

Most days, she did her best to forget her husband's final day, choosing to remember her husband as he'd lived, rather than as he'd died.

Ethan would've wanted it that way.

***

She'd met Ethan when she was fifteen. He'd come to Davenport on a farming mission, intent on trading tips with the locals. Or so she'd been told.

She'd been living with her aunt and uncle at the time. Several years earlier, Ella's parents had died from Winter's Death, a severe outbreak of the flu that had claimed fifty lives in Davenport. In addition to thinning the population, the illness had stripped the town of knowledge. Many of the deceased had been farmers or tradesman, and their absence left a gap in the economy, leading to a long season of famine.

And so Ella struggled. In addition to mourning her parents, she had to move out of her childhood home. Aunt Jean and Uncle Frederick were kind enough, but it was an adjustment, and one that didn't come easy.

With the arrival of Ethan, everything changed once again.

On that particular day, her aunt and uncle called her in early from the field. Ethan was waiting in the house. Ella immediately scanned the table, certain she'd find a display of crops, but there was nothing but the boy, smiling nervously. Ella looked at him, confused. It wasn't until she saw the expression on her uncle's face that she understood.

"This is Ethan," Uncle Frederick said.

His eyes watered, and he cleared his throat. Although Uncle Frederick was normally stoic, he was unable to contain his emotion. When she finally digested what was happening, Ella darted out of the house without a word, running into the field as fast as her legs would carry her.

Tears sprung to her eyes as she plowed through the grass. She kept her gaze on the harvest fields, intent on gaining as much distance from the scene as possible. Although she suspected this day would arrive, she hadn't thought it would come so soon. There were things she had to take care of here — one obligation in particular that it broke her heart to leave with her aunt and uncle.

After several minutes of running, she collapsed into a ball in the field, crying quietly into her hands next to a row of leafy squash plants.

Several minutes later, she heard footsteps.

Ella hugged her knees, praying she could make herself disappear. With the exception of one happy miracle, the past few years had been some of the worst of her life, and she was still getting adjusted. When she looked up, she expected to find the stern face of her uncle, but was surprised to find Ethan. He knelt down on the dirt.

"Are you okay?" he asked.

The boy kept his distance, watching her from several feet away. She noticed his eyes darting around the landscape rather than looking at her, and after a while, she relaxed.

"I think so," she answered.

As she looked over at him, she realized she'd barely taken him in. Ethan's hair was brown and shaggy, his eyes a penetrating blue. He was handsome. Although he looked several years older than her, he had the appearance of someone who was just as confused as she was.

"My parents sent me here," he confessed. "They're waiting for me at the market."

Ella nodded, drying her eyes. "I guess I won't be picking the rest of my crops."

Ethan went silent for a moment, the guilt apparent on his face.

"You can, if you want to."

"But they'll need me to—"

"Never mind. I'll help you finish."

With that, Ethan got to his feet and walked down the row, locating a half-filled basket of squash she'd left behind. He brought it back to her and helped her to her feet, then gave her a smile.

"You'll have to show me which ones are ready," he said.

"You don't already know?" Ella wrinkled her brow in disbelief.

"Sure, but you might do things differently in Davenport. I'm from Brighton."

With a coy smile, he bent over the nearest plant and made a show of tugging at the green leaves. Ella watched him for a minute, and then, unable to contain her amusement, walked over and showed him. Soon they were pulling squash together, filling the basket.

"The soil in Davenport is difficult for planting," Ella said.

"How so?"

"My aunt and uncle had to work around the rocks. It's hard to find dirt that is deep enough."

"That makes sense. The villages built too close to the ruins are often that way," Ethan said.

"What's it like in Brighton?" she asked.

"Mostly the same. My parents have a farm, sort of like this one. The soil is rich for vegetables. I'm getting ready to purchase my own plot. I've been saving for it since I was a boy."

"How old are you?"

"Almost sixteen. My birthday is just after the harvest."

They chatted more, speaking of the yearly festival and the annual Riverwash, as well as the merchants they knew in town. Before long, they were laughing and getting along, and Ella forgot that her aunt and uncle were waiting for her. When they finished filling up the basket, Ella stopped in the field, glancing back at the house she'd called home for the past few years.

"I guess we'll have to head back in."

Ethan's smile faded, and she saw that he was just as nervous. "Yeah. I told your aunt and uncle I'd bring you back inside."

"How long will you be in town?" Ella swallowed.

"Just long enough to plan the ceremony." Ethan paused, his eyes darting back to the field. "That is, if you agree."

Ella's heart swelled with emotion, and she nodded, forcing back the tears. Although she didn't have a choice, she was grateful he'd asked. Unlike the older men in town—the ones who whistled and catcalled while she delivered vegetables, she sensed that Ethan was different. And even though they'd just met, she was able to envision a life with him.

The illusion of choice was better than having no choice at all.

Chapter 34: Ella

As promised, Ethan secured his own plot in Brighton, and a year later, William was conceived.

Although she was homesick at first, Ella thrust herself into her new routine, tending to the newborn baby and assisting with the crops. Ethan's parents helped in raising William, filling in the gaps left by Ella's aunt and uncle. Soon the memories of her past life in Davenport faded — except for one that haunted her and another she treasured — and her life transitioned into something she could describe as happiness.

Ethan proved himself a hard worker, producing more food than was necessary to survive. Although a surplus of silver in Brighton was a rare thing, especially among The People, it was a goal Ella and Ethan both shared. As they tended the fields and delivered crops to the merchants, they dreamt of a day when they could lighten their workload.

Because travel was dangerous and expensive, Ella lost touch with her aunt and uncle, seeing them only a handful of times over the years. She did her best to fill William's head with tales of her uncle's firm but pleasant face, her aunt's talent for cooking and sewing.

Despite the threat of demons and the periodic anxiety of The Cleansing, much of the last decade had been a pleasant one. Up until Ethan's parents got sick.

The plague was vicious, and by the time it ended, it claimed the lives of her in-laws. Although Ella, Ethan, and William managed to escape the illness themselves, they spent the majority of their earnings on roots and medicines, hoping to assist Ethan's parents.

And the worst was yet to come.

Right before the harvest, Ethan was called into battle. The soldiers had detected a horde of demons close to the border, and they enlisted the help of the townsfolk. Many of the farmers protested, citing concerns about lost crops and unprotected families, but General Blackthorn ignored them. The General had only one priority—eradicating the demons.

Ethan left for almost a week. During his absence, Ella and William did their best to tend to the crops, confident they could get through it.

Ella could still remember the joy she'd felt when her husband had returned from battle. But instead of returning her affection, Ethan kept them at a distance, sharing little about what he'd been through. It wasn't until a day later that she found out the reason.

Ethan was infected.

Were it not for Ethan's confession, she wouldn't have known. Although it was rumored that many of the unclean were overtaken by delusion, Ethan was coherent, and she begged and pleaded with him not to turn himself in. But Ethan was resolved. He'd sworn to abide by the town's rules; he wouldn't see his wife and son killed for his mistakes. Before she could stop him, Ethan departed to see the town officials.

A day later, he burned.

Even now, Ella still bore guilt from his decision. Every time she looked at her son, she saw a fatherless boy, a boy as lost and alone as she'd felt in Davenport when her own parents had died. If she could've done things differently, she would've fought harder for Ethan to stay. She should've broken the town's rules; she would've found refuge from the unyielding brutality.

If she had, Ethan might've still been alive.

But even that wouldn't have protected her son.

Chapter 35: Ella

William was still scratching his neck when they reached the base of the mountain. A few seconds later, he turned his attention to the forest. Bray was slinking along, keeping cover between the trees, and he motioned for Ella and William to do the same. They followed his instructions.

Ella eyed the sheathed sword at her waist. She was still petrified to use it. What if she swung and missed? What if she lost her balance? She found herself wishing she'd paid more attention to the swordfights at the harvest festivals. If she had, she might've gained some insight on how to maneuver. For now, she was more comfortable with her knife.

She maintained a close eye on the forest around them.

Although they'd escaped the soldiers, there were bound to be others. Especially when the first batch didn't return to Brighton. She could only hope that the guards would relax their search. How long would they look for a lowly woman and child? Hopefully Ella and William would be able to hide until they were forgotten. It wasn't the greatest plan, but at the moment, she didn't have any others.

Although it'd been years since Ella had seen her relatives, she could still picture her aunt's and uncle's faces. The last time she'd seen Aunt Jean and Uncle Frederick had been when William was six years old. They'd come to visit Brighton. At the time, she and Ethan had been going through a difficult harvest, and her aunt and uncle had helped them. Uncle Frederick had lent her a hundred silver. Ella envisioned the coins in her bag and felt a twinge of guilt. She didn't have much, but when she got to Davenport, she'd find a way to pay him back.

Ella was hit with nostalgia, and she dabbed her eyes with the back of her hand. Her sleeve was covered in blood. She looked down at her dress. The entire garment was ripped, bloodied, and dirt-stained. Ever since leaving Brighton, it'd only gotten worse. Each encounter had left a mark on her, battle scars made of filth and fluid. She needed to clean herself off before reaching Davenport. She needed to clean William. Bloodstains would lead to questions, and questions would lead to capture.

Bray, on the other hand, could get away with his appearance. He was a Warden, after all, and they were expected to be road-weary. She'd have to make sure he knew to stop. Ella drew up alongside him.

"Will we be traveling near the river?"

"Not really," he said. "Unless you want to get caught."

"I don't think we should go into town looking like this."

He looked her up and down, as if assessing her condition for the first time. "I'll get you new clothes when we get there. But you'll need to pay me for them."

"Won't they have already seen us by then?"

"You can wait by the outskirts, and I'll bring them to you."

Ella pursed her lips, not quite satisfied with the answer. In her flurry to leave Brighton, she realized she hardly given enough thought to what they'd do when they got there. What if the soldiers arrived first? Surely the guard knew of her relatives in Davenport. Her hope had been to get a head start, seek out her relatives, and beg them to keep her hidden.

What other choice did she have?

Her mind strayed to worst-case scenarios. Davenport had the same rules about the unclean. What if her aunt and uncle turned her in?

She pictured the way her aunt and uncle had looked at William when they'd first seen him. He'd only been a few years old, then—barely old enough to toddle, and not yet old enough to talk, but they'd had taken an immediate liking to him. They'd even mentioned how nice it would be to live closer together. Ella had entertained the possibility for some time, thinking up plans to move to Davenport. But that had been before Ethan had gone to battle, and before he'd been burned.

Neither had come to bid Ethan farewell. It wouldn't have been proper.

It'd been five years since they'd visited Brighton. She swallowed her misgivings. Her first priority was getting to Davenport. She fell back from Bray and rejoined William. The boy was walking a few steps behind, and his eyes roamed from one side of the forest to the next.

"Are you all right, William?" she whispered.

He nodded, but she could see fear in his stare. She stopped walking and grabbed hold of him, suddenly fearful that he was losing his coherence. He stopped to look at her.

"Are you sure you're okay?" she asked again, more insistently.

"I'm fine."

"You look pale."

"I'm fine. Nothing's the matter."

She noticed he was avoiding her gaze. She gave him a motherly stare. A few seconds later, he let her in on his thoughts.

"Am I going to eat people, Mom?"

Ella bit back tears. She pulled him close and held him against her, listening to the steady throb of his heartbeat. How long would she be able to get this close to him? Would it be a day, a week, or a year? She opened her mouth to comfort him, but found herself choking back a sob instead.

Chapter 36: Ivory

After spending most of the morning on top of the mountain, Ivory backtracked for half a mile to a broad prairie. He spent the first part of the morning hunting for rabbits. Jingo would appreciate the gift. There'd be no rabbits in the ruined city. Ivory bagged several before he headed back for the cliff and found the trail that led down the mountain.

He zigged and zagged his way along the narrow path, careful to tread lightly and stay alert. At the slightest misplaced noise, he'd hide under a bush or behind a thick tree, far from the trail. The realm of the twisted men was not safe for anyone uninfected by the spore.

To be discovered was to risk death.

The trip down the mountainside was slow. But it always was. When in the demon's realm, one often had to choose between speed and caution. Ivory's uncle had taught him caution was always best. Keeping a cool head, thinking, and hiding were so much easier than running, and those skills had saved him countless times when he'd been unfortunate enough to come to the attention of a demon.

Working his way through the ruins was slow. Slow time passed while he hid, watching his surroundings, listening, and dashing to the next hiding spot—always in the shadows, always in underbrush. To walk the trails worn clear by demon feet invited disaster.

The fallen megalith was his goal. When his uncle was still alive, they worked together scavenging the enormous pile of rubble on every trip. As his uncle had explained, the most recently fallen towers had an abundance of accessible metals.

The other crumbled structures had either been picked clean by past generations of scavengers, or the exposed metals were more rust than usable steel.

It was almost midday when Ivory made his way up on the northern side of the giant mound. In the years since the building fell, he'd never scavenged this side. For whatever reason, he and his uncle had started scavenging on the southern side, and had eventually worked their way West. With all of the easily accessible metals gone from those two sides, Ivory decided to continue the pattern on the northern side.

Up on the rubble pile, he didn't worry too much about being spotted by demons. There were plenty of places to hide. He kept the same rules he held when working through the city—while scanning the area, he stayed out of view, and when he was sure that no eyes were on him, he stepped out and gathered the metals he'd spotted.

He was following that procedure when he stepped quickly across a long flat piece of old wood, assuming—badly—that the wood was simply lying across other rubble. Halfway across, he realized the wood felt soft underfoot. His first thought was that it might give way. He pulled his arms close to him in preparation for a fall. Better to land on a shoulder and get a bruise rather than stick out a hand to brace himself and snap a wrist.

Ivory's foot continued to sink. His leg was through a hole and up to his knee. He stomped his other foot down on the wood to catch his balance, hit rot, and the whole slab fell away beneath him. He reached out to grab something… Anything. But everything in his reach was falling too.

Ivory's feet hit something solid and uneven. He was off balance and not coming to a stop. Wood, rocks, and other bits of debris fell with him. He tumbled over big chunks of stone and down a slope, rolling and bouncing.

He collided with a floor of flat stone. Bruised, scraped and trying to catch his breath, he realized he'd stopped. Around him was darkness. High above him, sunlight poured in through the hole he'd created. He cursed himself for his carelessness. Stepping on that piece of wood was a mistake that could've killed him. It still might.

Ivory listened for the sounds of demons in the darkness around him. He heard nothing.

He waited and didn't move.

Not even small animals hid in the permanent shadows down here. Or they did and they were frightened into silence by the intruder.

Birds twittered in the air outside.

Ivory was sure he was alone.

He sat up and wiggled his fingers and toes. He bent his elbows and knees. Then he took a deep breath. He touched his hand to his head. He'd gotten a good bump while tumbling. Only a tiny bit of blood came back on his fingers. He'd gotten lucky. Nothing seemed broken, and nothing was bleeding—at least not bleeding enough to worry over.

Peering into the darkness, Ivory got to his hands and knees, then to his feet. Despite years of ancient dirt and fallen debris, the floor was well preserved, patterned in an array of colors and designs—all finer than anything he'd seen in Brighton and covering the entire space around him. When the building above had collapsed all those years ago, it must have left a cavity, a great banquet hall a hundred feet across, with sloping walls of rubble and a ceiling supported by nothing that Ivory could make out in the gloomy shadows high above.

With his eyes following the pattern on the floor to where it disappeared beneath the rubble, he tried to make out what the pattern represented. Did the plants, animals, and curving lines represent anything? Probably not. Few things the Ancients constructed made any sense.

If the building above hadn't collapsed, creating barriers of debris, Ivory wondered how far he could have walked in this subterranean realm. Could he have traveled all the way through the Ancient city and to the borders of the town? Ivory laughed at himself for such a silly idea. Still, he liked to imagine what life had been like in the time of the Ancients, before the ruins, before the demons.

He sighed as he noticed a glint of metal in the rubble that surrounded the floor.

It was time to turn his tumble into good fortune. Confident that he could quickly make the climb back up to the surface should he come across anything dangerous, he chanced a walk lightly along the edges of the floor, perusing the wall of crushed old stone, broken glass, and pieces of metal. Some of the pieces were so large they'd be impossible for him to remove, even with the help of a dozen men.

Along with the giant beams of steel and rusted ropes — ropes that seemed to grow right out of the broken stone — pieces of rare metal were mixed all throughout the debris mounds. Ivory saw hard steel, the kind for swords, broken into pieces small enough to load into his bag. He also found steel that didn't hold an edge for long, but never rusted. He found pieces of aluminum, light and permanent. It was no good for making cutting weapons, but it was a prized material for making spear shafts, and it was highly prized for arrow shafts like the ones in his quiver. Those arrows flew far and true. Much better than wood.

The blacksmiths back in Brighton eagerly bought those metals, turning them into all manner of tools and weapons. Although the metals were contraband — going to the Ancient city was forbidden, after all — the blacksmiths didn't acknowledge their origin, and Ivory didn't speak of it.

Ivory contemplated exploring further, but put the thoughts out of his mind. He needed to get moving if he was to get to Jingo's. Without delay, he collected as many pieces of metal as he could easily carry in his bag.

Ivory took one final glance at the trove of metals in the rubble all around and made his way carefully up the pile of debris to the hole through which he'd fallen. When he climbed out, the sun was higher in the sky. Ivory took his time scanning the ruins around him, making sure he was alone. He covered the hole with pieces of large debris, ensuring they were strong enough to be walked across. He didn't want some wandering demon discovering the cavern by accidentally falling in just as Ivory had. If that happened, his discovery would get turned into a warren full of stinking monsters. His trove would be lost.

When his stash was hidden, Ivory worked his way back down through the rubble, heading in the direction of the tower where Jingo had made his home.

Chapter 37: Ella

"How far?" Ella asked.

Bray was several steps ahead of her. They'd been trekking all morning, and it felt like they were getting close to Davenport. In spite of that, Ella's memory was far from trustworthy; it'd been years since she'd made the journey, and distances seemed much different now than they'd seemed in her childhood.

"Not far," Bray affirmed. "When we get close, you'll see the tops of the buildings over the trees. We should be there by midday."

Ella felt a swell of relief. Since leaving Wanderer's Peak, she'd been expecting the worst—bands of soldiers lurking behind every cluster of trees, packs of demons springing from all directions. So far, the journey had been quiet. Ella had spent much of the time ruminating on the events that had occurred over the past few days, reliving the choices she'd made. She assumed there'd be many days like that to come. She was surprised she'd even been able to sleep in the cave.

Her brain flashed to images of the soldiers she'd stabbed in Brighton—blood spraying from wounds she'd inflicted, groans emanating from opened mouths. She tried to recall the rousing speeches she'd heard given to soldiers before they marched off to battle. She'd never been a part of them, but she'd eavesdropped. The soldiers trained on a field several streets removed from town, and she'd passed by while making her way to the merchants. The leaders spoke of courage in battle—about giving up one's life for the protection of the townsfolk, about making decisions fearlessly.

Wasn't that what she'd done?

She didn't believe the town's teachings—that women were weak, and that only the hardest hearts could prevail. The noblest people she'd encountered were those that were not only able to fight, but also to feel. People like Ethan. People like her uncle. Those were the people she aspired to be like, and those were the people she wanted William to admire. For as long as he lived, she'd impress those values upon him.

She was so caught up in her thoughts that she almost didn't notice the forest deaden. The transformation was subtle. At first, the birds stopped chirping, then the insects ceased their chatter. The wind died. Ahead of her, Bray stopped, as well, and was holding his blade at the ready. Ella scanned the forest.

Something was close by. She could feel it.

The air had taken on a fetid odor—a stench that permeated her surroundings and almost made her gag. She pressed a hand to her mouth, holding her breath to avoid taking it in. Beside her, William did the same. She knew the smell.

Demons.

Around Ella were trees and underbrush, but in the distance, she could see the light of a clearing. Bray gazed through the trees. After surveying the forest for several seconds, he put a finger to his lips and beckoned them onward.

They snuck to his side. With each step, the smell thickened, as if the scent were a ghost and they'd walked into its embrace. As they approached the clearing, Bray sank to a crouch. Ella and William mimicked his posture.

Several hundred feet across the clearing, shapes, hunched and lump-covered, crept through the grass. If Ella didn't know better, she might've mistaken them for primitive animals grazing in an open field.

"Stay still," Bray said.

Ella wanted desperately to run, but she obeyed the Warden. As much as she distrusted the man, he knew the ways of the demon. And out in the wild, that knowledge was greater than currency.

The infected were moving in the opposite direction, surveying the knee-high grass. Although their movements were erratic, the longer Ella stared at them, the more she could pick out a pattern. Several creatures were leading the group, as if they were generals of some infected band of troops, directing their men through the terrain.

Ella looked over at Bray, trying to swallow her fear. "What are they looking for?"

"Us, most likely."

"They know we're here?"

"Possibly. Either that, or someone else is passing through."

"Can they smell us?" William asked.

"I don't think so. Their senses are the same as ours. They're probably surrounded by the same stench." Bray wrinkled his nose. "The only difference is, they probably like it."

The creatures swayed back and forth. Every once in a while, one of them cranked its head and stared back at the forest, and Ella ducked low and held her breath.

"We should be fine," Bray assured her. "We'll just wait them out, and then we'll adjust our path. It looks like they're heading west."

Ella peered over at William, who was taking in the scene intently. It was as if he were watching his future unfold. She wondered if he envisioned himself out in the open field. She'd protect him from that. She'd rather die than let him roam the wilderness like an animal. If it came down to it, she'd even…

She couldn't think about that.

Ella swallowed the lump in her throat. William had turned to Bray, and she could see the curiosity on his face. It seemed like his fear had abated.

"How many skins do you think are out there?" He smiled.

"Forty-two," Bray said.

William held up his finger and quietly counted the air. "You're right. How'd you know that?"

"Lucky guess."

Bray smiled at Ella, but she scowled and looked away. William was recounting, as if the Warden might've played a trick on him.

"Have you ever fought that many at once?" William asked.

"Not that many," Bray said. "But close."

"Did you defeat all of them?"

"Yep. I got thirty-five skins that day."

"How'd you manage to do it?"

Bray smirked, unable to disguise his pride. "Do you want to know how?"

William nodded anxiously. Ella kept her eyes on the field, but found herself listening intently. Despite her mixed feelings toward the Warden, any knowledge he could impart would be worth having. Their survival might depend on it.

Bray gave one last look over the field, and then continued. "It happened about a year ago, right after the Brighton soldiers defeated a horde outside the walls. The demons had grown scarce, and many of the Wardens decided to head out past the frontier into the deep forests. I figured I'd head south. Most of the other Wardens were heading west, so I figured I'd have better luck in another direction. As you probably know, not many people have ventured that far away from the three towns, and I wasn't familiar with the area. One morning, as I was coming down from my camp on a mountain, I stumbled on a pack of infected. They were trolling a field at the mountain's base, scavenging among the trees. Because of the direction of the wind, I hadn't smelled them, and by the time I saw them, they'd already spotted me."

Bray paused for breath. William stared at him, eagerness in his expression.

"I turned, ready to flee, but I was butted up against an incline, and I knew that if I tried to run, I'd be overtaken. There was nothing I could do but fight them off. It took me a good part of the afternoon to slay all of them."

"How'd you do it? How'd you kill them?" William asked.

Bray scratched his chin. "There are certain things you learn along the way—strategies that become instinct. Things you don't know until you're faced with a situation like that," he said evasively.

"But don't you have certain methods? Like the soldiers do?"

"I have my ways."

Bray stopped and reached for his pack, watching Ella and William. He pulled out a flask of water and drank from it, letting his cheeks billow with the liquid. Ella felt a swell of annoyance. Rather than say anything, she held her tongue. When Bray was finished, he inspected the field and then resumed speaking.

"You want to know my secrets?" he asked.

Ella and William nodded.

"For one, never stop moving. The minute you stop moving is the minute you die. The demons have a difficult time catching a moving target. If there are a number of them, they tend to trip each other up, so you can use that to your advantage. Chase them from side to side, and attack the fiercest ones first. Never let yourselves get surrounded. In this particular instance, I had the mountain at my back, which limited the number of ways they could approach. If you get surrounded, you're as dead as the soldiers we left on the mountain."

Ella nodded her head, processing the information. William's eyes were big and round, staring at Bray in amazement.

"You said it took an afternoon to slay them?" he asked.

"Almost," Bray said. "When I'd thinned their numbers, I was able to lead several of them away and dispatch them individually. By that time, I'd decided I wasn't going to flee. The prospect of silver was too good."

"What happened when you defeated them all?"

Bray wiped his lips and returned his water to his pack. "Afterwards? I headed to The House of Barren Women and took a nice, hot bath." He grinned.

Chapter 38: Ella

When the demons had disappeared from the field, Bray led Ella and William in another direction, avoiding the open grass and heading deeper into the woods. Rerouting would lengthen their journey, but it'd give them a buffer zone from the creatures.

After a few minutes of traveling, the smell started to dissipate, but Ella could still detect the odor in her mouth and nose. It was a stench she'd always equate with death. As persistent as it was, she was glad it existed—it warned them of danger, and it probably saved their lives.

They hiked for a while longer without speaking, and she could tell William was searching for the creatures. He held his knife in hand. Several times, when he thought no one was looking, she caught him taking a practice jab. She recalled his ambitions as a child. At different points in his young life, he'd wanted to be a soldier, a merchant, and a farmer. Although she wasn't fond of some of his phases, she'd never squashed his dreams. As Ella knew from her own childhood, one's aspirations would change over time, and there was no use dwelling on the fleeting whims of a child. It was best to let him explore the world around him, finding his own passions and his own path.

The realities of life would dissuade any child soon enough.

She pretended not to see William swinging his blade, letting him have his moment. Bray wove through the trees at a rapid pace, and Ella and William fought to keep up. It was evident he knew the forest as well as anyone, and she was once again grateful to have him as a guide. Most of the journey guides she knew, though knowledgeable about the wild, weren't skilled in battle.

Bray possessed both attributes.

At one point, she heard the distant roar of the river, and she envisioned the demons drinking from its banks. In just a day, she'd learned more about the wild than a year of listening to stories in taverns could've taught her.

Most of the people in Brighton were isolated and removed, dependent on the teachings of the ministers. The only knowledge they had was from stories, and many of those stories were full of embellishments and mistruths. She'd always suspected this, but she'd never dared give voice to her theories.

Now that she was seeing things firsthand, many of her suspicions had been validated. The only way to learn about the wild was to immerse oneself in it, as dangerous as it was.

As the sun climbed higher in the sky, William began to stumble. Ella reached out for his arm to steady him.

"Are you okay, William?"

He stared at her with guilt in his eyes. "I'm hungry," he confessed.

Ella felt a shimmer in her heart—the feeling of a mother who'd been neglecting her child. They hadn't eaten since yesterday. Regardless of their hurry, they could afford to take a moment. "Let's stop."

At the sound of their conversation, Bray turned back and walked to join them. Ella shrugged the pack from her shoulders and opened it, pulling out an apple she'd taken from the soldiers. She handed it to William, watching him devour it hungrily. Then she withdrew some berries for herself. She was tired of the taste, but happy to be fed, at least.

"If we weren't in a hurry, I'd catch us some game," Bray offered. "But we need to get moving."

Ella agreed. She finished her meal and washed it down with water. It was getting towards mid-day, and the sun bore down from overhead, splashing light through the trees. The birds and insects were as vocal as ever. It was as if the animals had forgotten the disruption of the demons, and were reclaiming the forest.

William stared at Bray as he chewed.

"What are the buildings like in Davenport?" he asked. "Do they look the same as the outskirts of Brighton?"

"Some are taller. But you can't climb inside them. They aren't safe, and they're covered in weeds," Bray answered.

"Most are forbidden," Ella agreed.

"Do the kids go inside them anyway? Like they do in Brighton?"

"William!" Ella scolded. "You know better than that."

"I haven't gone in, myself," he said, turning his head to disguise the lie.

"You better not have," she warned. "And you won't be exploring the ones in Davenport, either."

"I can't wait to see them, that's all."

"Who says you have to wait?" Bray asked.

Ella and William turned to ask for clarification. Before they could speak, they saw what Bray was referring to. Deep in the distance, over the tops of a few trees, were the tips of several majestic buildings.

"Welcome to Davenport," he said with a smile.

Chapter 39: Ivory

The sky was bright and yellow when Ivory arrived at the base of a tower that stood twenty layers tall. Each layer was the size of a prairie, and he could walk through most of them without bumping his head on the layer above. Each was lush with plants around the edges and filled with small animals. Birds perched and nested. In the center of each layer, where the suns rays never fell, they were barren caves.

Vertical columns cut through the layers. Some were empty shafts that fell away to the ground. Others held the rusted remains of stairs, in places sturdy, in some covered in plants and shrubs, and in still others, fallen away over time, to leave gaps that couldn't be crossed.

No stairs allowed for climbing from bottom to top. The tower was a maze. Ivory made his way up through a few layers on stairs that were intact. In one of the empty shafts, he climbed the rusted rungs of an old ladder. That was only good to get him past another three layers. Eventually, he had to climb on the roots and branches that grew between several floors, putting him outside the tower and in danger of falling a hundred feet to his death.

As he navigated the building, his mind wandered. He thought about The Cleansing. He was glad he'd missed it again. He'd seen enough bloodshed during his days to scar his nights forever. His uncle had been taken from him years ago; to this day he could still hear the man screaming. If it weren't for Ivory's father, Ivory would consider leaving the town and its walls behind. The wonderment of the ruins and the quest for knowledge beckoned with far more vigor.

He switched focus to the loot he'd taken, and the coins he'd make when he traded his metals in Brighton. For the millionth time, Ivory considered the possibility that he might one day come across a treasure trove of coins—ancient coins. If that happened, he'd have no need to collect metals for selling to the smiths. He'd only need to pretend to be a hunter of limited talent. He was surprised nobody had figured it out already. Anybody paying attention would know that his trips into the forest ran for way too many days and that he always returned with too little game. Anyone paying attention would know that the house where he and his father lived—where they used to live with Ivory's mother and Ivory's uncle—was more house than could be afforded on the income from Ivory's and his father's hunting.

Eventually, Ivory reached the highest layer, which had a roof overhead. He worked his way across the building. His thoughts of Brighton faded. His focus was on the coming few days, and the knowledge he'd gain while in the ruined city. Ever since his uncle had started taking him here, he'd found purpose far greater than anything in the township could have offered. He stepped over the familiar juts and holes in the ground, working his way to a more stable area on the far side, one that would serve as his home for the next few days. He could already make out the far outer wall of the building. There, at the edge, watching over the ruined city, sat Ivory's friend and teacher.

Jingo turned. His silhouette against the gleaming sun showed the calcified warts on one side of his head as he said, "Hello, Ivory."

Chapter 40: Ella

At the sight of Davenport, Ella and William hastily finished their meal. As she closed her pack, Ella kept her eyes glued to the treetops, as if the tips of the buildings might disappear. A part of her was convinced that the town was an illusion, and that she'd wake up again in the cave, listening to the sounds of demons feasting on human remains.

But the buildings were real.

Her eyes watered as she took them in. She recognized several already—ancient and looming, their tops crumbled, but holding. Although time had dimmed the details, the buildings looked familiar, as if she'd never left.

"Come on, William!" she said.

She tugged William along, keeping after Bray. Now that she'd seen Davenport, the forest seemed less menacing. It was as if the town itself was a repellent against the demons, and its mere presence would protect them. She had to remind herself that they were still in danger. The men in Davenport were just as apt to condemn them as those in Brighton, whether she reached her relatives or not. Though death would be less imminent, it would be no less severe. Their best bet was to immerse themselves in the town and find her aunt and uncle.

The last thing they needed was to arouse suspicion.

Ella reviewed her plan in her head. Her goal was for Bray to get them clothes, then sell her wares and seek out her relatives. If something went afoul, she'd have the silver and could seek refuge in another town.

The plan was far from foolproof, but right now, it was the only plan she had.

As she hiked after Bray, she prayed he'd be able to get them inside undetected. Showing up through the gates so soon after a Cleansing would arouse suspicion. Her memory of the town was almost twelve years old, and many things had likely changed since then, so she'd need to depend on him.

As she strode through the forest, she pictured the town vividly: the streets colorful and vibrant, the sound of merchants, traders, and children punctuating the air. She remembered walking those streets with her parents, holding their hands as they strolled past the vegetable stands and parked wagons. That was before the plague, and before the troubles she'd had at her aunt's and uncle's. Everything seemed more prosperous then. Whether it was the innocent gloss of childhood or her own naiveté, she didn't know, but the memory was comforting.

William deserved to have memories like that. She'd make sure he had them.

As the buildings in the distance loomed closer, Ella noticed Bray had sheathed his sword, and she followed suit. It was always wise to stand down while in the vicinity of a settlement. Entering town with a weapon drawn was an easy way to get oneself killed. From what she recalled, there was a wall on the east side of Davenport, but she wasn't sure if that was where they were headed. Bray had changed course several times; her bearings were lost.

"Which way are we going in?" she asked.

"Normally I'd take you through the east wall, but there'll be too many guards there. I know another way — a path between buildings that'll bring us closer to the merchants."

"Won't they see us?"

"Not if we're careful."

She refrained from further questions, content to follow Bray. William scurried closer to her. He'd never been to another of the towns before. Although she'd meant to take him, he'd been too young to travel. It was a shame they'd come under these circumstances.

Ahead of them, Ella could see the light of a clearing. In just a few feet, the thick underbrush had relented, and the outlines of buildings sprung into view a few hundred yards away. The sight of Davenport proper made her heart gallop.

Ella listened intently, expecting to hear voices. She could already read evidence of civilization on the ground—broken underbrush, the beginnings of paths, and boot prints in the dirt.

Bray stuck to the outskirts of the forest, keeping them out of plain view. As they crept through the trees, she tried to separate the buildings from the groping hands of nature, discerning what had once been the ruins of the Ancients. The walls of old buildings had long outgrown their function, and served as barriers to keep the town contained.

And somewhere inside those walls were the people she'd come to see. Somewhere inside were Aunt Jean and Uncle Frederick.

She bounced between excitement and fear. How would her aunt and uncle react when they arrived? Would they agree to help? What if they cast her away? She couldn't imagine them betraying William. Ethan had been one matter, but a child? She swallowed. Every possibility needed to be considered.

There was a chance they'd be forced to flee. There was a chance the Brighton soldiers would catch up to them. Hell, there was even a chance her relatives would try to have her burned. If that happened, she'd fight her way out of Davenport, she'd get William to safety.

They were approaching the back wall of a building. Bray pushed aside the overgrowth, exposing the dirt-worn exterior. The building was covered in clumps of ivy, but he cast them aside until he'd revealed a hole in the wall. Through it, she could see the crumbled interior. Beyond the building, through another hole in the far wall, she saw a dirt road.

Bray put his finger to his lips. "Stay here," he said.

"Where are you going?"

"To see one of the merchants. He should be able to help us."

"What's his name?" Ella asked, as if she might remember him.

"Elmore," Bray said.

She didn't recognize the name. "He'll pay us for the scalps?"

"Yes, and he'll have clothing for you, too."

Ella paused. "Are you sure we can trust him?"

"No. But I won't tell him any more than he needs. When I crawl through this hole, follow me, but stay inside the building. When I'm finished, I'll come get you." Bray held out his hands for her pack.

"I don't think so," Ella said. "The pack stays with me."

"How will I sell your things?"

"We'll accompany you."

"In that condition? Not a good idea."

Ella looked down at her clothing, still stained in blood. She gave Bray a hard stare. Although she'd trusted him to take them this far, the memory of what he'd done to them in the cave was still fresh. She couldn't—wouldn't—allow him to take her things.

Bray chortled. He gave Ella a long look, then turned his attention back to the hole. "How about this? Give me three bits of silver to get your clothes. When I have them, I'll come back and get you, and we can return to the merchants together. But you'll need to wait in the alley."

Ella reluctantly agreed. She tugged off her pack and removed three bits of silver, handed them to him, and watched him disappear through the hole.

Then she sucked in a breath and followed him through. William stayed close behind.

The building was dark, damp, and unoccupied. What was left of the floor was covered in rubble and weeds. Ivy clung to the walls and ceiling, as if the forest had slowly been working its way inside. She scanned the dark walls and the corners, ensuring no one was lurking within. Then she stared out of the hole in the far wall at the dirt road.

She recognized the area. Although time had made subtle changes, she was able to pick out several landmarks—a short building with a cracked door, a taller one with a misshapen roof. A row of wagons waited outside the latter, probably awaiting vegetables from the harvest.

The road was quiet. There was no one in sight. She'd expected to hear the bustle of the townsfolk, but the street was oddly empty.

She looked over at Bray, who was standing next to them in the darkened room. In the time she'd been distracted, he'd quietly drawn his sword.

"What's wrong?" she whispered.

He didn't answer.

The Warden crept through the building for a better look at the street. Ella felt a sudden sense of foreboding, one that slid through her body and wormed its way through her joints. A minute earlier, her primary concern had been encountering the guard or being apprehended by the Brighton soldiers, but now her thoughts had taken a new direction. Where was everybody?

William grabbed hold of her arm. "Mom? What's that smell?" he hissed.

"I'm not sure," she whispered.

She knew what it was. It was the odor of death, and it clung to the air like a cool breeze, wafting over the town.

Bray crept through an opening in the building and onto the street, beckoning for them to follow. With each step, Ella expected to hear the din of voices, the cries of children at play, but there was nothing. The town was silent. It was as if all of the townspeople had packed their belongings and left.

She held her sword in her hand and kept William close by.

They traveled the narrow road, expecting to be stopped at any moment by the guard, or a merchant, but the only greeting they received was the occasional caw of a bird. The buildings were their only companions, and the moss-covered walls seemed as ancient as they ever had. Ella's legs felt tingly and numb, as if something had crawled inside her and taken control. She recognized more and more buildings as they walked, but each one only fueled her unease. All of them were empty. All of them were lifeless. They were approaching the center of town.

They took a turn, entering one of the main roads that led to the square.

Ella immediately covered her mouth, bile threatening to spill from her stomach. The mangled remains of the townsfolk were everywhere. Women, children, and soldiers had all been torn apart with equal abandon, mouths hanging open, limbs mangled. Merchant stands—once filled with fruits and vegetables—were toppled, the hay carts overturned and shattered. The carcasses of pigs were strewn about the street, as if their entrails were the last touch in some perverted parade.

The blood in the road was sticky and wet, and Ella sidestepped to avoid it, as if interacting with it would make the scene real. But it was real, and no amount of avoidance would make it go away.

The entire town had been massacred.

The dirt-covered roads, once filled with life, were now carpeted with the blood and bones of the people who'd once walked them. Ella clutched her son with a shaky hand, as much to hold herself up as him.

"Wh-what happened, Mom?" William whispered.

She shook her head. There were no words for the scene. The carnage on the mountain had been a mere taste of what was to come, a foreshadowing of the violence they saw now. Who could've done this? Was it the demons? A rogue band of soldiers? No one else would be able to reap so much suffering. She surveyed the scene for some evidence, but found herself more confused. Some of the townsfolk had been stabbed, but others appeared to have been torn apart and eaten.

There was no reason to the madness.

She took a step forward, almost tripping over the gutted body of a merchant, his entrails coiled around his neck, his tongue lolling from his mouth. A strangled woman lay next to him, her neck purple and bruised. Each spectacle was worse than that last, and each scene was something out of a nightmare.

They needed to get out of here. They needed to leave.

But she was unable to move. It was as if the spectacle had rooted her in place, preventing her from doing anything but taking it in.

Bray walked several steps ahead of them, swiveling from one building to the next, as if whoever—or whatever—had attacked the town would leap out and grab them. But the town was deathly silent.

There was no evidence of the perpetrators.

She pictured her aunt's and uncle's faces, smiling as they played with William, bouncing him on their knee. They were gone. Even without seeing them, she knew. She choked on her tears. She'd check for them, of course, but she knew…

Bray walked back to join them.

"What happened?" she whispered, hoping he'd have an answer.

"I'm not sure," he said simply.

"Who could've done this?"

Her face stung with tears. The Warden didn't answer. For the first time since she'd met him, she could tell Bray was afraid.

TO BE CONTINUED…

Read on for a Preview of Book 2 out Winter 2014!

PREVIEW: The Last Survivors (Book 2)
Chapter One: Ella

They were dead. All of them.

Ella didn't need to count the bodies to know that all three hundred of Davenport's residents had been slaughtered. She reached out for William, but her son had already broken away, and he stepped among the gutted and the strangled, his mouth stuck open in disbelief.

"We need to get out of here," Bray urged.

But Ella's feet were frozen in place. She scanned the faces of the dead townsfolk, thinking she might recognize someone. A few were familiar, but it was impossible to tell for sure—their expressions were twisted in the throes of death, their features marred with blood and gore.

"Ella!" Bray hissed, louder. His sword was out, and he spun in a slow circle, as though the perpetrators might reappear. But nothing moved. The village was empty. The smell of blood was thick and fresh enough that even scavenging birds and rodents hadn't dared venture out yet.

Ella imagined the cries that had filled the air, the panic that must've ensued before the massacre. How could this have happened?

"We can't leave," Ella whispered, still in shock.

"But we have to—"

"I need to find my aunt and uncle. I need to find…"

She broke from her trance and darted down the street, collecting William. She leapt over toppled pushcarts and spilled vegetables, holding onto his hand, pushing the images of gore from her mind almost as soon as she saw them. Her feet had taken over for her mind, leading her from one turn to the next, operating on muscle memory and adrenaline. William heaved thick breaths beside her. He didn't speak, not even to question her.

Anywhere they ran was better than here.

She heard Bray's footsteps behind them as he chased, but he'd ceased calling for them. The village was silent save the clap of their boots, the world as small as the butchered streets before them.

Ella flew by building after building, barely taking in the sights. Doors hung open with no one behind them. Houses stood vacant. She'd never seen the village this quiet. Except for The Cleansing, of course. Had The Cleansing already happened? It must have. It was an unbreakable tradition.

This must've happened after.

But none of that mattered. All that mattered to Ella was following her feet and her memory, making her way to the place she'd once called home. With each street they passed, the carnage thickened. Bodies were sprawled in every direction. Not just the remains of the townsfolk, but the remains of animals, as well, butchered and half-eaten. They'd have to run through the square to get to her aunt and uncle's.

Things would get worse before they got better.

Her stomach heaved and churned. But she wouldn't stop until she'd reached her aunt and uncle's. In the distance, about a hundred feet away, she saw the steeple of the worship building, the place where she'd spent many days in her childhood. The peak rose a hundred feet in the air, the walls built from the smooth gray material of the Ancients. The structure was as majestic as she remembered it.

Davenport had been built around its remains.

We're almost there, she thought, as though reaching the village center would somehow erase the chaos. But her body gave away her fear. Her heart slammed against her ribs; heavy gasps burned her throat. She dodged the body of a slain merchant, catching a glimpse of his gouged eyes and the hilt of a knife protruding from his forehead. So it hadn't been demons. Not all of it.

Men had done this.

She barely had time to register the thought when she'd rounded the next corner. She flew past the worship building, giving way to an open, dirt square about several hundred feet across. Bodies lined the edges, many with spears in their backs. Women and children and the elderly had been killed with equal abandon.

Two heads were in the center on spikes.

The ministers, she thought. As she ran, her mind conjured the images of Father Towson and Father Decker, who'd come to Brighton for visits and guest sermons. She hadn't particularly liked them, but they didn't deserve to die. Not like this. None of this made any sense.

Tears spilled down her face.

With William running behind her, she dashed across the square, approaching the slain ministers. The sticks were propped several feet above the ground, displaying the severed, ruined faces for all to see. The alley to her aunt and uncle's was in view, just past the village center; she'd have to pass the spiked heads to get to it. As she approached, she felt William's hand go slack in hers, and saw that he was staring at the ministers. Unwittingly, she followed his gaze.

Only the heads didn't belong to the ministers.

Ella stopped running, an icy numbness working its way through her body. She hadn't recognized any of the bodies so far. Not through the blood and gore. But she recognized these.

She clasped her hand over her mouth, unable to contain her sickness. Staring at her from the tops of the spikes, their eyes sightless, their faces splashed with blood, were the severed heads of Aunt Jean and Uncle Frederick.

"No!" Ella wailed, collapsing to her knees. She turned her head and heaved into the street. William fell to the ground next to her, grasping her arm. He was crying, too. He would've remembered them. They hadn't visited in five years, but there was no mistaking their relatives.

She closed her eyes and reopened them, hoping to find proof that this was all a dream, but it was real. The death and the destruction of Davenport was total and irrevocable.

Bray drew near, his face sympathetic. His eyes wandered from the spikes and then back to Ella. "Blackthorn," he said.

"What?" Ella dried her face and looked up at him. She furrowed her brow, as much in disbelief as in mourning.

"Blackthorn did this to get to you. To send a message."

The words hit her like a punch to the stomach, and the tears were flowing again, and she was powerless to stop them. This was all her fault. She'd avoided The Cleansing; she'd skirted the will of The Word. And now others had paid.

"No," she managed.

"This wasn't because of you," William said next to her. "It was because of me." He dried his face and got to his feet. She watched him through a veil of tears. His face was contorted in both anguish and anger. How could she comfort him? There was no way to mend what had happened.

To her surprise, he raised his fist in the air and began to shout. "I'll kill you! Do you hear me?"

"Quiet!" Bray said, grabbing the boy's arm.

William ignored him. "I'll kill you, Blackthorn!"

The boy had lost control, and he writhed in Bray's arms. Ella leapt to her feet. She grabbed hold of William's other arm, doing her best to hush him. His face was flush and streaked with tears. After a few seconds they were able to settle him down. She looked across the bloodied square, certain she'd find a band of soldiers, but the square was empty. Even still, they needed to get out of here. But not yet.

"I need to check on something else," Ella said.

"This isn't wise. We have to—" Bray began.

"Please." She gave him an insistent stare and then started for the other side of the plaza. Bray and William followed. She scoured the ground as she ran, tracing the faces of the fallen townsfolk again. Soon she'd reached the alley past the square. The buildings were small and close together, and her mind jumped to memories of her youth. She'd played chickenball and rattles in the streets, just like William. She'd had friends. She'd had dreams. The scenery was so familiar, and yet so wrong.

She stepped around the bodies of several women lying facedown in the dirt, their dresses hitched above their waists, made to look indecent even in death. She glanced inside several open doorways, hoping she'd see someone inside, a survivor of the massacre, someone who could explain what had happened. She needed hope now more than ever. But the small houses were dark and empty.

Four doorways further was the entrance to her aunt and uncle's. She recognized the door even before she was upon it, and she picked up her pace until she'd reached it. Stomach hitching, she crossed the threshold.

The house had been ransacked. Her aunt and uncle's bedrolls were slashed, their storeroom raided. A sack of grain lay empty in the corner, the contents dumped across the room. The floor was wet and it reeked of urine. If there was any resemblance to the place where Ella had grown up, it was lost in the disorder.

Her eyes flitted across the ruined room. She walked inside and picked up the blankets and bedrolls. Then she went to the storeroom and peered inside. The shelves were barren, the contents either stolen or destroyed.

"What are you looking for?" Bray asked from the doorway, his sword at the ready.

Ella didn't answer. Her heart was pumping furiously.

"Take some supplies, if you must," Bray added. "But be quick about it. They'll be back looking for you. We can't stay."

Ella ignored him, growing nauseous again. She walked to the entrance, pushing by Bray, and scanned up and down the alley. But there was no sign of what she was looking for. She turned around to find both Bray and William watching her.

"What are you doing?" Bray asked.

"I was hoping she was still here," Ella said, tears in her eyes.

"Who?"

"I was hoping I'd find my daughter."

Blatantly Begging for Reviews

We are really hoping you enjoyed our first collaboration, and hoping that you can help out a couple of indie authors by giving a few minutes of your time for a quick review.

Just in case you weren't aware, here are the actual benefits of reviewing books by indie authors:

Prevent some 5th avenue publishing exec from buying a new yacht or seventh home in the Hamptons

You will be blessed with 72 virgins (it's like a scavenger hunt…you'll still have to find them!)

You will amaze and entertain your friends and family

The prestige of having your words published online for the world to see (yes, it's really fun!!)

You'll get a free pony*

(* just kidding about the free pony)

Okay, no, seriously…when you leave a review, it helps push books up into the "popular books" lists on Amazon, where more readers find out about them…it really helps new authors compete with the mega-conglomerate publishing companies, allowing guys like us to ditch our corporate jobs and follow a dream.

If you loved (or at least liked) the book, thanks for taking a chance on us. We both appreciate it. Please take a moment to leave a few words about what you liked about The Last Survivors at the following link:Thanks!

Bobby, T.W.

If you REALLY liked the books and just can't wait to hear more about upcoming releases:

Here are the links where you can sign up
for each of our email lists:

T.W. Piperbrook: http://eepurl.com/qy_SH
Bobby Adair: www.bobbyadair.com/subscribe/

About the Authors

T.W. Piperbrook

T.W. Piperbrook was born and raised in Connecticut, where he can still be found today. He is the author of OUTAGE and the best-selling CONTAMINATION series. In addition to writing, he has also spent time as a full-time touring musician, traveling throughout the US, Europe, and Canada. He lives with his wife, a son, and the spirit of his Boston Terrier.

Facebook: www.facebook.com/twpiperbrook
Website: www.twpiperbrook.com
Email: twpiperbrook@gmail.com

Other Works by T.W. Piperbrook:

CONTAMINATION SERIES:
Contamination Prequel
Contamination 1: The Onset
Contamination 2: Crossroads
Contamination 3: Wasteland
Contamination 4: Escape
Contamination 5: Survival

Save money and start with the Contamination Boxed Set (Books 0-3) at a discounted price!

OTHER WORKS:
Outage

Bobby Adair

Where I'm from and who I was isn't important except to say that I'm pretty much just like you. I worked lots of years in shit jobs (actually most of them paid pretty well) that I hated. But it finally occurred to me one day that it wasn't the jobs that were bad, it was me. I did my time at the widget factory because I was too lazy to chase my dreams.

Well, one day, I got off my ass and I did chase them.

Now, after a lot of work (still going on) here I am. I'm a writer. I don't say that to brag. I only say it as proof, but if I can go over the wall and follow my dreams, you can too. It ain't easy, but it's worth it.

Facebook: www.facebook.com/BobbyAdairAuthor
Website: www.bobbyadair.com/subscribe
Pinterest: www.pinterest.com/bobbyadairbooks/
Twitter: www.twitter.com/BobbyAdairBooks

Other Books by Bobby Adair

THRILLER:
Ebola K: A Terrorism Thriller

HORROR: SLOW BURN
Slow Burn: Zero Day, book 1
Slow Burn: Infected, book 2
Slow Burn: Destroyer, book 3
Slow Burn: Dead Fire, book 4
Slow Burn: Torrent, book 5
Slow Burn Box Set: Destroyer and Dead Fire

SATIRE: Flying Soup

Text copyright © 2014, Bobby Adair & T.W. Piperbrook

ALL RIGHTS RESERVED. This book contains material protected under International and Federal Copyright Laws and Treaties. Any unauthorized reprint or use of this material is prohibited. No part of this book may be reproduced or transmitted in any form or by any means, electronic or mechanical, including photocopying, recording, or by any information storage and retrieval system without express written permission from the author/publisher.

This book is a work of fiction. Any resemblance to actual persons, places, or events is purely coincidental.

Printed in Great Britain
by Amazon